Venus
Spring

Jonny Zucker writes for children, teenagers and adults. His first novel for Piccadilly Press was the teen title *One Girl, Two Decks, Three Degrees of Love*, which was serialised by BBC radio. Jonny lives in North London with his wife and young children. FInd out more at www.jonnyzucker.com

Venus Spring

Star ✪ Turn

JONNY ZUCKER

PICCADILLY PRESS • LONDON

For Isaac

First published in Great Britain in 2007
by Piccadilly Press Ltd,
5 Castle Road, London NW1 8PR
www.piccadillypress.co.uk

A catalogue record for this book is available
from the British Library

ISBN-13: 978 1 85340 902 8 (trade paperback)

1 3 5 7 9 10 8 6 4 2

Printed in the UK by CPI Bookmarque, Croydon, CR0 4TD
Cover design by Simon Davis
Cover illustration by Nicola Taylor
Animation drawings by Polly Holt
Typesetting by Carolyn Griffiths, Cambridge

Set in 11 point Palatino and Avant Garde

FRIDAY

The cobbled alleyway was lit by narrow shafts of moonlight as the unmarked van purred to a stop at its entrance. In the back were the country's top teenage military cadets, male and female. They sat in absolute silence, their eyes locked on Corporal Adam Lester. He glanced at his sleek silver watch and eased open the back doors of the van.

'GO!' he hissed.

Swiftly and noiselessly, the combatants streamed out of the van, their guns pressed close to their chests, their legs striding over the ground. The future of the entire country rested on how well they performed in the next thirty seconds. But as they sprinted through the alleyway, their movements were suddenly halted. They completely froze in mid-stride.

Stunt co-ordinator Ed Fry pressed a button on the DVD remote and the pictures of the teenage soldiers vanished from the screen.

•• | ••

'That's where you come in,' Fry explained, pointing to a large diagram tacked to the wall, marked with several red circles. 'From that second on, you lot are in the frame – everyone running in unison. You take the corner and head for your positions in the barracks. Are there any questions?'

It was six p.m. and fourteen-year-old Venus Spring looked around and had to suppress a squeal of excitement. At three-thirty that afternoon, her school had broken up for the autumn half-term. She'd said goodbye to her mates and headed straight over to Elstree Studios. And there she was, sitting in a large room at the film studios with a group of teenage stunt artists. They had been rehearsing a storming-the-barracks scene for the last couple of hours, ready for the shoot the next day.

Venus had dreamed of doing real film stunts ever since her stunt man granddad, Dennis Spring, had started teaching her stunt skills years ago. What had started off as a wish to spend time on film sets with Dennis had turned into a desire to become a fully qualified stunt artist. She'd even attended Dennis's stunt camp in the summer holidays to learn more skills – but had ended up thwarting a conspiracy to poison the local countryside, with the plotter dying in a plane explosion and Venus thinking she'd killed the plotter's son, Franco. That name still sent shivers down her spine. Contrary to her initial belief, he was very much alive and had warned Venus he was after her. Venus tried to put all thoughts of Franco out of her mind whenever they strayed there.

In the past when she was on film sets with Dennis, she'd only been allowed to do stunts when there was a break in filming and the set was in 'dead time'. Yet there she was going over the final preparations for the real thing – her first action movie stunt. And what a film to be in – *Airborne Sword 2!* Dennis had been the stunt co-ordinator on *Airborne Sword* which was hotly tipped for massive success, and had got some tickets for the premiere the following weekend.

Dennis had been asked to do the job again on the sequel, but he had had other commitments, so Ed Fry had got the job of directing the second unit – which was the team responsible for filming all of the scenes that didn't involve the main actors – instead. This included the stunt scenes – and there were plenty of those.

And Venus was there because of Elliot Nevis.

Elliot was Venus's estranged father. He'd shown up on a Sunday night six weeks ago. Venus had just walked into Dennis's apartment, when a figure emerged from the kitchen.

'I'm Elliot Nevis. I'm your dad.'

Those six words made Venus feel like she'd just been

punched in the solar plexus. There suddenly seemed to be no air in the room. Her head was filled with a mesh of emotions: anger, fear, elation and confusion. *This* was the unravelling of the central mystery in her life? This man with cropped blond hair and almond-shaped green eyes – the one she'd looked at a million times in the one grainy photo she had of him – was her father? She couldn't see a resemblance; she had the same large brown eyes and lush brown hair as her mother, though her skin was a lighter coffee colour and her body more toned due to her kick-boxing and athletics. She didn't want to be a waif or a fashion-clone; she needed to keep fit because of her stunt ambitions.

Venus fixed her gaze on Dennis, and at that moment her usual bright expression was replaced with a shaky look of uncertainty.

'Is he?' she asked tentatively. 'Is he my father?'

Dennis nodded uncomfortably.

'Look, Venus,' said Elliot softly, taking a step towards her, 'I really am your dad. There's a lot to explain and —'

But before he could finish his sentence, Venus took a step backwards and found her voice. 'How dare you use the word *dad!*' she snarled at Elliot, her brain threatening to go into meltdown. 'You walked out on Mum and me when I was THREE MONTHS OLD! What sort of a dad does that?'

Her body shook with years of pent-up rage. This was the man who'd deserted her and her mum, Gail. He was the one who'd deprived her of having a two-parent childhood. How many hours had she spent wishing that he'd never left them?

'What the hell makes you think you can just suddenly turn up in my life and "explain" everything?' she yelled. 'It's way too late for that!'

'You only know part of the story,' said Elliot quietly.

'You've been in touch with him, haven't you, Granddad?' asked Venus, suddenly turning to face Dennis again.

Dennis blushed, a real rarity for him. 'It's been very hard, Venus; we've always had to think of you.'

'Think of *me*?' Venus snorted with derision. 'No one seems to have thought of me. I'm the one who's been kept in the dark.'

Dennis reached out and put his arm on her shoulder, but she pushed it away and turned back to Elliot.

'All right then,' she said, seething, 'put me out of my misery. Tell me the truth.'

'It's long and complicated, Venus,' Elliot replied, 'and I *will* fill you in on the details. But for now I just want you to know that I didn't simply walk out on the two of you – I had my reasons, very good reasons; in fact, staying was impossible.'

'Why?' demanded Venus. 'What was so impossible?

Was having a baby too overwhelming for you? Couldn't you bear the sleepless nights or something? You must have really hated Mum and me to do that to us.'

Elliot shook his head. 'No, Venus, I didn't hate either of you, quite the opposite, but elements elsewhere in my life had spiralled out of control and things became too . . . difficult.'

Venus took a deep breath and changed tack. 'Does Mum know you're here?'

'No,' Elliot replied, 'and at this stage I'm not going to tell her. The split was very traumatic for both of us.'

'Traumatic!' shouted Venus. 'You ran back to America, left her with a tiny baby and never got in touch again! That doesn't sound very traumatic for *you*!'

Tears streamed down Venus's cheeks. She'd waited so long for this moment, but now it was here, it wasn't the sunny reunion she'd dreamed about. It felt twisted and uneasy.

'It wasn't like that,' Elliot replied, his voice breaking.

'Well, what was it like?'

Elliot sighed heavily. 'I've tried to contact Gail many, many times over the years,' he explained, 'but each time, she's told me to stay away from both of you.'

Venus was bewildered by this. Her mum had always said that Elliot just suddenly dumped them and then completely vanished from their lives. She couldn't help wondering if he really had tried to contact them over the years or if it was just part of some charm offensive. She stole a glance at Dennis.

'It's true,' Dennis whispered, his face shadowed by emotion, 'and, like Elliot said, it's very complicated.'

'Well, why are you seeing me now?' Venus asked, turning back to face Elliot, her voice losing a sliver of its edge. 'What's changed?'

'I've stayed in touch with Dennis throughout these last fourteen years,' Elliot replied. 'I had to. Your mum wouldn't see or speak to me, but Dennis kept the channels of communication open. He's filled me in on how you're getting on. I've wanted to see you so many times, but I promised your mother I wouldn't. However, two weeks ago, I was asked to come to London for a special assignment. I haven't been back in all this time, but I decided I'd reached a turning point. Venus is fourteen now, I told myself. I've respected Gail's wishes for all this time, but now I think you are old enough to make your own decision about whether or not you want to know me.'

Venus was completely floored. It felt like her whole world had just been fractured. She massaged her temples to try and dislodge the hammering pain inside them.

'Well, what kind of assignment is it?' she asked, feeling

she needed to get away from the personal stuff for a moment.

'It's connected to the film industry,' Elliot replied.

'In what way?' Venus couldn't help being interested, in spite of herself.

'I've been hired by a very wealthy English family called the Cribben-Taylors,' Elliot explained. 'They invest very large sums of money in films. When a film they've backed does well, they make a lot of cash; when a film bombs, they lose money. The Cribben-Taylors are the main backers of the *Airborne Sword* trilogy.'

Venus raised an eyebrow.

'*Airborne Sword 2* is being filmed on location in England over the next couple of months,' Elliot continued. 'They're up in Liverpool for four weeks, and then Manchester for three weeks. The last week is being shot here in London, based at Elstree Studios.'

'What's the problem?' asked Venus.

'The Cribben-Taylors have once again acquired the services of Scott Marshall as producer/director. As you probably know, he did *Airborne Sword*. Being producer and director means he not only directs the actors, he also controls the budget – it's a massive job.'

Venus knew what a producer/director did. 'So?' she asked.

Elliot pursed his lips. 'Unfortunately, having initially

been delighted to get him after the great job he did on *AS1*, the Cribben-Taylors now think that Marshall is stealing money from them.'

'So why don't they just sack him and get someone else to do the job?'

'Because they have no evidence; if they sack him without any proof, he'll sue them and they'll end up paying millions in compensation.'

Venus frowned. 'Er . . . what's any of this got to do with you?'

'The Cribben-Taylors have hired *me* to find out if Scott Marshall is up to no good and if he is, to get some proof.'

Venus paused for a second. She remembered that she didn't actually know what job Elliot did. Her mum had once said he was employed by the US Government, but she hadn't given any details.

'Are the Cribben-Taylors connected to the United States Government?' she asked.

Elliot looked puzzled. 'No,' he replied. 'They're hiring me off their own backs.'

'Well, how long are you going to be in England?' Venus asked. 'Is it weeks or months or . . . ?

'I'll be in England for a week.'

In the end, Elliot spent a very frustrating week in Liverpool. Scott Marshall had decreed *Airborne Sword 2* a completely closed set. Unless you were directly involved in the film, you weren't allowed anywhere near it. A team of ultra-vigilant security guards made sure of this.

Elliot had phoned Venus every night. Once, her mum nearly answered her mobile for her, but Venus had just managed to dive forward and grab it before she did, imagining how terrible it would be if her mum found out she was in contact with Elliot behind her back.

Initially she was freaked out by these calls and felt her anger rising the second she heard his voice. But however furious Venus was with Elliot, a part of her wanted to make the most of any time she had with him, even if it was only on the other end of a phone. She'd asked several times if he'd be coming back to England after this one week, but he'd been frustratingly evasive.

Over the course of these phonecalls, he filled her in on some basic details of his life, like where he lived (an apartment in Manhattan), what he got up to at weekends (watching baseball games and jogging in Central Park), and if there was anyone special in his life (there wasn't). In turn she answered his questions about school, her mates and her kick-boxing.

It became clear to Venus that although she looked like her mum, personality-wise she was actually more like Elliot. Her mum was a lawyer and very into the whole legal set-up, but Elliot was more into sport and games, just like Venus.

In the last of these phonecalls, he'd told her he'd been called back to the States on another matter. He apologised for leaving so abruptly and promised he'd be back soon. He said he'd stay closely in touch.

On his past performance as a father, she took these promises with a massive dose of salt. But, true to his word, he phoned Venus twice a week from the States and however vague he remained about the past, she felt like she was getting to know him a tiny bit better as the days passed by. She was still angry with him, but she was beginning to feel that he perhaps wasn't just a selfish, arrogant man who'd walked out on his partner and kid. She was sure there had to be more to his story than that, even if he wouldn't give her all the details.

Dennis was very concerned about the whole Elliot situation. It was very difficult for him as he wanted to be loyal to his daughter. But he did say on more than one occasion that he was relieved that Venus had finally met her father.

'We'll have to let your mum know at some stage,' he warned Venus one evening. 'However angry she'll be, she's got a right to know.'

'You're right,' said Venus, nodding, 'but not yet. Maybe when she's less busy with work.'

Elliot remained in the States for three weeks and then announced he was heading back to the UK, to have another go at the Scott Marshall situation. The filming of *AS2* had moved to Manchester and he had some good contacts up there, but unfortunately their help wasn't good enough. If anything, the security around the set had been tightened and he returned to London after just two days in Manchester, frustrated and gloomy.

Dennis, Elliot and Venus sat one evening in Dennis's living room, with Elliot bemoaning his failure. They looked at any new possibilities that could get him near enough to Scott Marshall to see what was going on, but they kept on drawing blanks.

After a long silence, an idea suddenly popped into Venus's head. She sat upright, her face intense with concentration.

'I've got it,' she announced.

Elliot and Dennis looked at her enquiringly.

'You know you said the last week of *AS2* is being filmed in London?' she asked carefully.

Elliot nodded.

'Well, that's my half-term week. I'm on holiday,' she continued, 'I'll be around.'

Elliot fixed her with an intrigued stare. 'I don't get it,' he said.

'It's simple,' said Venus, her eyes suddenly alight with the potential of her scheme. '*You* haven't been able to gather any evidence on Marshall, but maybe *I* could.'

Dennis coughed. Elliot looked bewildered.

'You said that part of the London week of filming is about a military youth academy, right?' asked Venus.

Elliot nodded.

'So there'll be quite a few stunts during that week's filming, won't there?'

'Yes,' agreed Dennis slowly.

'And those stunts will be performed by teenagers, yes?'

Elliot suddenly saw where Venus was heading. 'You're not serious?' he said.

'I'm totally serious,' replied Venus enthusiastically. 'With Dennis's contacts, I'm sure I could get in there. It's the only way you'll get anywhere with this Marshall guy.'

'Look, it's a very kind offer,' said Elliot, 'but it's not on. This is my responsibility, not yours.'

'Think of it as teamwork,' insisted Venus, who was getting surer of her plan by the second.

'Stop right there, young lady,' said Dennis, waving a finger, 'There's no —'

'Just hear me out, Granddad,' Venus cut in, fixing him with a resolute expression. 'You were the stunt co-ordinator on *AS1* and Ed Fry is doing that job on *AS2*. You and Ed go back years – he's one of your oldest pals.'

'Yes, but it's a ridiculous idea,' said Dennis. 'Even if I did phone Ed, he'll have had all the stunt people in place months ago; you know the kind of planning this work involves.'

'Surely you could ask him a favour?'

'That's not the point, Venus,' Dennis sighed.

'Of course it's the point, Granddad! It'll be brilliant! I'll get on to the set, do my stunts and have a snoop around Marshall when I can. Give Ed a call and see what happens. Please?'

Dennis took a deep breath and blew out his cheeks. He knew how stubborn his granddaughter could be.

Venus turned to her father. 'I'm not just doing this to help you, Elliot,' she said. 'It's good for me too. It'll give me the chance to do my first *real* film stunts. Come on – it's the perfect solution.'

Elliot and Dennis glanced at each other uncertainly.

'I . . . I don't know what to say,' said Elliot.

'It *would* be a great experience for you,' murmured Dennis, 'but if Marshall is up to no good, it might be dangerous.'

'It won't be dangerous!' protested Venus. 'It won't be like dealing with Franco and his mum, or those nutcases who kidnapped me and Tatiana.' Venus had experienced plenty of action in the last couple of months.

'Who's Franco?' asked Elliot.

'He's just some boy I met at Dennis's stunt camp,' replied Venus.

'He's a bit more than that,' countered Dennis.

Before Elliot could ask more about Franco, Venus dragged

the conversation back to her grand plan. 'And I'll be very subtle,' she said. 'Marshall will have no idea I'm checking up on him. It makes perfect sense,' she said. 'Come on!'

Neither man replied for a good minute.

'I suppose you have a point,' muttered Dennis cautiously. 'You *are* ready for your first real stunt . . .'

Venus threw her arms round Dennis. 'Yesss!' she cried.

'Hang on a second!' exclaimed Dennis. 'I haven't spoken to Ed Fry yet.'

Venus hurried across the room and returned brandishing a cordless phone.

'Are you sure about this?' asked Elliot anxiously.

Venus gave him a firm nod. She pressed the phone into Dennis's hand.

Dennis leaned back in his chair and gave the proposal another couple of minutes' thought. Finally, after frowning intensely, he punched in some numbers on the handset.

'Hey, Ed, it's Dennis. I need to ask you something about *Airborne Sword 2*.'

Dennis asked Ed Fry if Venus could join the stunt team for the week's shoot in London, talking up Venus's abilities as a stunt girl and how she was ready for an on-screen challenge.

Fry had met Venus a couple of times and had been impressed watching her practise stunts with Dennis, and told Dennis that his timing was immaculate. It turned out that someone had withdrawn due to an injury at the last minute, so there was a space in the stunt team.

When Dennis had put the phone down and told them the news, Venus couldn't believe her luck; this was her big chance to prove herself under real movie-making conditions – her dream!

Elliot was amazed by her feisty endeavour and thanked her several times for going in – partly on his behalf. 'My long-lost daughter might find out something that I can't,' he said, smiling gratefully. 'But there's no pressure on you, Venus. If you don't find anything, that's fine; just don't take any risks.'

'Yes,' added Dennis gruffly. 'Any snooping you do will have to be quick, clean and totally secretive. If Ed Fry or anyone else finds you poking around, you'll be off the set in seconds. Do you get me?'

'No worries, Granddad.' Venus beamed. 'I'll only go looking if there's no risk of being spotted.'

'Good,' replied Dennis, 'but there's a lot of legal stuff and paperwork to be sorted out before we get the full green light. So bear with me. I'll get cracking on it straight away.'

Like all of Venus's previous experiences of learning and performing stunts, she and Dennis decided not to tell her mum the whole truth. Venus told her she was spending half-term on a film set to watch and observe close up, but not that she'd actually be *performing* stunts herself. Gail Spring wanted her daughter to follow her into law, and Venus was pretty sure Gail would highly disapprove of her stunt ambitions. Venus knew she'd have to tell her one day about her dream to be a stunt artist, but felt that day was still a long way off.

So that was how Venus got to be at Elstree Studios, brimming with excitement and sitting with her fellow teen stunt cast members, listening to Ed Fry getting them ready for the next day's stunt shoot.

The army barracks had been impressively constructed by a huge team of set designers and technicians. The whole thing looked very realistic from the front, but Venus had walked round to the back of the barracks and seen there was nothing there. It was literally a façade, but as façades went it was pretty amazing.

The stunt team's job began at the point where Fry had stopped the DVD; just after the young soldiers piled out of the van and began to race through the narrow alleyway. The actors and actresses who were playing the teen soldiers were the ones in the van and the ones who entered the alleyway. Up to that point the camera tracked them from the front, showing their hardened, determined faces. However, as they sprang out of the alleyway and in the ensuing fight scene, Venus and the other young stunt artists would take over and the camera would mainly track them from behind. They were all dressed in combat gear, so to the casual eye there would be no difference.

The stunt team were needed for this scene because the soldiers' mission was to storm the army barracks at the far side of the square. This would involve lots of running, jumping and diving through sugar-glass windows. However good the actors were, none of them was qualified to do any of this.

Fry spent over three hours putting the stunt group through their paces, from the second the camera picked them up to the point where they would crash into the barracks. Venus knew it was necessary to get these things absolutely spot on, but by the end of rehearsal she felt that if she had to do the run another time, she'd go completely mad.

All the while though, she was very conscious of the main reason she was here on set – to investigate Scott Marshall. She'd been tempted to start asking some of the production team about his movements, but she didn't want to appear too inquisitive on her first day. She'd begin her enquiries the next day.

Back home, after eating supper with her mum and talking vaguely about her day spent on the *AS2* set, Venus popped round to her best friend Kate's.

'So how was it?' demanded Kate, flicking on her iPod and selecting a mellow playlist for background music. 'Any cute boys?'

Venus laughed. 'Why would I be thinking about cute boys? Jed's coming down in a few weeks.'

Jed was the gorgeous guy she'd met at stunt camp; the same boy who was coming down to London the week after next. She'd get to hang out with him for the whole of Saturday afternoon and most of Sunday.

'At last you'll have time together again!' Kate grinned. 'Are you going to tell him about your dad?'

Venus shrugged her shoulders. 'Maybe.'

'Are you still feeling guilty about seeing Elliot behind your mum's back?' asked Kate.

'Totally. It's *so* weird. But I can't tell her. She might flip out and stop me ever seeing him again; it's too much of a risk.'

Kate thought about this and nodded. 'OK then, what about tomorrow? Your big day – your first ever proper stunt! Are you all set?'

Venus swallowed nervously. Despite all the run-throughs, just *thinking* about the army barracks shoot made her feel incredibly anxious.

'I can't believe it's actually happening,' she murmured.

'You'll be fine,' counselled Kate, 'you've been trained

by the best, haven't you?'

Venus nodded, but didn't quite share Kate's optimism. This was finally her big break. *Can I pull it off? Or am I going to mess up, big time?*

SATURDAY

'I've got a meeting with two of the barristers from that big burglary case, Venus.' Gail Spring addressed her daughter while she frantically searched under a sofa cushion for her mobile phone.

Venus looked up from the breakfast table. 'But Mum, it's *Saturday*,' she replied, holding up her mother's mobile, which had been hiding under a newspaper.

'Thanks,' said Gail, snatching the phone.

'You said you were going to stop working on weekends,' Venus pointed out.

'I know,' replied Gail between mouthfuls of toast, 'but I'll only be a few hours. What are you up to?'

Venus shook her head. 'I'm hanging out on the set of *Airborne Sword 2* today, remember?'

'What time will you be back?'

'Nine p.m. at the latest,' responded Venus.

'Dennis will drop you off as usual, won't he?' asked Gail, stuffing some papers into her bag.

'Yes, Mum.'

Venus hadn't told Gail that Dennis *wasn't* going to be on set this time. She would be bound to make a fuss if she knew this.

'I should be in well before then,' said Gail.

'I thought you said the meeting would only be a few hours?'

'It will,' Gail said, suddenly looking guilty. She felt bad about leaving in such a hurry, but there was loads of work to be done on the case. She gave Venus a peck on the cheek, snatched up her bag and hurried out of the house.

'OK, everyone, listen up.'

The *AS2* stunt co-ordinator, Ed Fry, beckoned for everyone to move in. The teenage stunt artists shuffled forward. Venus felt a strong pulse of excitement. The bright autumn sun shone down on the street in which the mocked-up-army barracks had been built. It was quite warm for October and runners were busy moving odds and ends off the set – a chair leg here, a mannequin over there. Venus was standing with three other members of the stunt team – Indigo, Brad and Hazel – all in their combat gear.

At seventeen, Indigo was the eldest of all the teen stunt artists. She came from a stunt family – her dad was a stunt artist – and Indigo had done seven movies. She had light green eyes, long light brown hair and high cheekbones.

Brad, sixteen, was five-foot-ten, with classic Australian good looks – blue eyes, a square jaw and a muscular body. However, unlike some good-looking boys Venus had come across, he was not at all arrogant and constantly put himself down, but in very funny ways.

Hazel had a short brown bob, wide dark brown eyes and a tiny snub nose. She was sixteen too and talked really quickly – Venus thought she seemed like a lot of fun. Hazel had done four films before, like Brad.

When Venus had told them the day before that this was her first film, none of them had laughed at her or patronised her as she had feared. She didn't let on that she was only fourteen – she'd always looked and acted older than she was, and if they thought she was sixteen, she was fine with that. Indigo, in particular, had gone out of her way to make Venus feel at ease.

'You're a natural,' Indigo told her on their final run-through before filming started. It was a small comment, but it kept Venus's nerves at bay a bit.

Venus hadn't yet told any of them that Dennis Spring was her granddad, because they might think she got the job solely because of him and not because of her abilities, which to be honest, was partially true.

'At least we're not kung fu pigs,' muttered Brad, casting his eye over to the barracks and then to Ed Fry.

'Why, have you been a kung fu pig?' asked Venus.

'Yeah,' Brad replied, turning back to face Venus. 'I had to do this fight scene with a half-monkey, half-reptile creature called Gravel. It was bizarre!'

Venus laughed.

'How are you feeling before your first real stunt?' enquired Indigo.

Venus shrugged her shoulders. 'The truth?' she asked.

Indigo nodded.

'I'm very, very nervous,' Venus replied.

'That's good,' cut in Hazel. 'I'm *always* nervous, but that adrenaline kick pushes you to give your best performance.'

'You reckon?' asked Venus.

'I know,' said Hazel, nodding. 'It's the same with everyone, even the actors who've starred in fifty films. Some of them get terrible stage fright and have to work extra hard just to get on the set.'

'So it's not just me?'

'No way,' said Brad.

Venus let out a sigh of relief.

'Anyway,' added Indigo, 'it's a top team on this film. I've done a couple where we had to work hard to carry some people's shoddy work – know what I mean?'

Venus nodded. Some of the people at Dennis's summer stunt camp had been brilliant; others were happy just to coast, doing the minimum amount of work possible.

Venus wasn't some stunt swot – she just badly wanted to make it in the profession and was willing to put the time and effort in.

'We're getting the studio bus to Pine Lodge later on,' Indigo said. 'You know, the hotel where the crew are staying. We're going for coffee; fancy coming along?'

Venus's ears pricked up. 'Are *all* of the crew staying there?' she asked casually.

'Most people,' replied Indigo.

'What, like even Scott Marshall?' enquired Venus.

Indigo laughed. 'He's got the biggest suite in the whole place – apparently it's the size of Wembley Stadium!'

'And he's got the biggest Winnebago on site!' piped up Hazel.

Excellent! thought Venus. *Two useful pieces of information.*

Venus had actually seen Scott Marshall earlier that day, standing next to a fake military van, looking extremely edgy. His face was pinched with exhaustion and tension.

Maybe it's just the pressure of producing and directing, Venus mused. *But then again, maybe it's not. Is he skimming off loads of cash from the Cribben-Taylors' budget? I need to crack on with checking up on him – I'll see if there's an opportunity tonight.*

'I'll only ever be truly happy when I have my *own* Winnebago,' Brad was sighing.

'Dream on!' said Hazel, laughing as she gave him a friendly punch on the shoulder.

'So are you going to join us or what?' asked Indigo.

'Sorry?' asked Venus, snapping out of her contemplations about Scott Marshall.

'For a coffee,' prompted Indigo, 'at the hotel?'

'Yeah, that's great,' said Venus, grinning. 'I'll come along.'

Indigo smiled back and, at that moment, Ed Fry's voice boomed across the street. 'Five minutes!' he called.

Suddenly, everyone around Venus began psyching themselves up. Brad started limbering up and doing stretches, Hazel was jumping from foot to foot, and another boy looked like he was meditating.

Venus looked towards the alleyway entrance where she and the others would burst into the square. They had to run across the square straight towards the barracks. Venus's route would take her towards the left-hand side of the building. She had to run up two sets of ten steps and then dive forward through a sugar-glass window – the type that was safer to use for stunts. The other cadets would be heading for their own assigned entry point or going down under gunfire.

'QUIET ON THE SET!' someone called.

Venus felt the adrenaline pumping round inside her.

This was really it!

'And CUT!' yelled Ed Fry.

Venus stepped out through the splintered barracks

windowpane she'd just dived through, expecting Fry to be delighted with her and the rest of the crew.

But he wasn't.

'Venus and Hazel, over here please!' he called.

The two glanced at each other uncertainly and hurried over to him.

Fry spoke in a low voice. 'Hazel, you moved too early; Venus, your angle of entry was wrong.'

Venus was stung with shock. She was sure she'd got it right.

Hazel was clearly stunned too. 'But I timed it perfectly,' she protested.

'Hazel, are you the stunt co-ordinator on this film or am I?' demanded Fry.

'You are,' muttered Hazel.

'What did *I* do wrong?' gulped Venus with dis-appointment.

'I wanted a ninety-degree turn before the second flight of steps. You were totally out.'

Venus frowned.

'Right then,' said Fry. 'Venus, stick to the angle; Hazel, move two seconds later. You can call me a perfectionist, but I know what I'm doing. Now off you go.'

As they walked back to their starting positions in the alleyway, Venus felt as if she'd just had a giant slap in the face.

My first stunt and I got it wrong! I can't believe it! Ed Fry will be cursing Dennis for agreeing to his request. What a total nightmare!

As she reached the entrance to the alleyway again, Indigo came over. 'Hey, Venus,' she said, 'I know what you're thinking. You're thinking "This is the end of my stunt career", aren't you?'

Venus took a deep, disappointed breath. 'How did you know?' she mumbled forlornly.

'Because I made a mess of *my* first proper stunt and I've been in six other films since then. That's what starting is all about. Fry won't hold it against you – just relax and you'll get it right this time.'

Venus was grateful for Indigo's reassurance, but she was worried that Fry would be cursing her, and that made her terrified of messing up the second take.

However, on the second take a light fuse blew before they reached the barracks. On the third take, a boy called Carlos knocked down one of the alleyway walls. Thankfully, the fourth take met Fry's brutally high expectations. Venus hit the steps and crashed through the sugar-glass window to Fry's satisfaction.

When Fry finally shouted, 'IT'S A WRAP!' Venus felt relief flooding through her veins.

'No one will ever remember that first take,' said Indigo, as she and Venus walked over to the catering van. 'All they'll see is the final scene, and that will look amazing.'

The Pine Lodge Hotel – a fifteen-minute drive from Elstree – had a white, stucco entrance and a marbled lobby that branched off into a wide corridor, which in turn led to the vast Clipper Lounge. The lounge was dotted with round oak tables, its walls adorned with oil paintings of giant trees. Across the entire far side of the room was a chrome bar, staffed by four men in immaculate black shirts. The lounge was heaving with members of the *AS2* crew, relaxing after a hard day's labour or working their laptops and Blackberries furiously, preparing for the next day. The air was filled with movie talk.

'Ed Fry's a hard taskmaster, isn't he?' said Hazel, as she, Venus, Brad and Indigo settled down at a table with coffees and a pack of shortbread.

'I've worked with him twice before,' said Indigo. 'He can be a bit over-zealous.'

'Are you sure he's not going to fire me?'

Indigo laughed. 'I told you earlier, Venus, you did really well today – didn't she, guys?'

Brad and Hazel nodded.

'For a first time, you were excellent.' Brad grinned. 'I broke my wrist on my first shoot. It was a low budget movie called *Oval Street*.'

'Seriously?' asked Venus.

'Yeah.' He laughed. 'I didn't even do it filming the scene. I fell off a stage before the cameras started rolling!'

The others laughed too.

'There was this really obnoxious boy on my first shoot,' confided Hazel. 'It was this Spanish film – *Night Fisher*. He was called Enrique. He was gorgeous, but a total pain in the backside. He was so intent on dominating the scene that the stunt co-ordinator had to remind him that he wasn't an actor – just a stunt guy!'

'Have any of you ever worked with Kelly Tanner?' cut in Venus. She didn't want to sound too starstruck, but Tanner – a brilliant American stunt woman – was her number one heroine. Venus was desperate to meet her, but so far Dennis hadn't managed to arrange it.

Indigo, Brad and Hazel shook their heads.

'She's amazing, though, isn't she?' said Hazel. 'People say she gets nervous like anybody else, but she'll take on pretty much any job – especially ones that other people are intimidated by. She's supposed to be a great laugh too.'

'It would be excellent to work with her,' agreed Indigo. 'She was going to be on the third film I did, *Canyon Mist*, but she pulled out at the last second.'

As the conversation quickly turned to the quarry explosion scene they'd be shooting, Venus sat back in her chair and thought about the day. Although she was still upset about her mistake, she did feel delighted that she'd done her first wrap. Hopefully it would be the beginning of many.

They talked some more, but when Brad was about to start yet another one of his film-world stories, Indigo stood up. 'I'm staying at a mate's house in Hammersmith and I need some sleep,' she announced, 'so I'm calling it a day. See you guys tomorrow.'

Venus, Brad and Hazel said goodbye and Indigo headed off. The three of them talked for a while longer and then they decided to head off too: Brad to his brother's place in Soho; Hazel to her aunt's house in Kensington.

Venus said she was just going to the loo and would see them both the next day. She headed in the direction of the toilets and waited round the corner until they had left. Quickly, she pulled a cream envelope and a black biro out of her jacket pocket. Neatly she wrote on the front of the envelope: *SCOTT MARSHALL. DELIVER BY HAND. STRICTLY CONFIDENTIAL.*

Holding the envelope, she approached the reception desk. A woman with scraped-back blond hair and wide, blue eyes smiled at her warmly.

'Good evening, madam,' said the receptionist, 'what can I do for you?'

'Er . . . it's about this,' replied Venus, holding up the envelope and revealing the writing.

The receptionist held out her hand to take the letter, but Venus pulled it back. 'I'm really sorry,' she said, 'but Mr Fry did ask me to deliver it personally.'

The woman's smile lessened a notch or two. 'We don't give out guests' room numbers,' she explained.

'I understand,' Venus said gently, 'but this is something really personal – I think it's from his wife.'

The receptionist wrinkled her nose and thought about this. She turned round, and for a moment Venus thought she was about to ask one of her colleagues what to do, but she made up her own mind. 'OK,' she said, leaning forward conspiratorially, 'it's Room 424, fourth floor. But don't tell anyone I told you.'

'Of course not,' agreed Venus solemnly. 'Thanks.'

Venus travelled up in the lift with two businessmen in sleek blue suits, who exited on the third floor.

Stepping out of the lift on the fourth floor, Venus followed a sign which said, *Rooms 420–440.*

After a fire door, she walked out into a long corridor carpeted in royal blue, with a series of wall lights at three-metre intervals. It smelled of freshly laundered sheets and polish.

Room 424 was on the right. She checked both ways down the corridor. Empty. Pressing her ear against the heavy door, she listened carefully. There was no sound coming from the room; no conversation, no TV, nothing.

Venus tried the handle. It was locked – no surprises there. She was standing by the door wondering what to do when she heard footsteps by the lifts. She turned round and felt her stomach lurch. It was Scott Marshall! He was striding down the corridor, talking on his mobile.

Venus threw herself forward and dived through a fire door. Her heart was beating wildly. Had he seen her? Might he recognise her from the set?

She stayed where she was, expecting him to come storming through the fire door at any second. But he didn't.

Venus wiped the sweat off her forehead and stepped cautiously back into the corridor. There was no sign of Marshall.

How will I ever get into his room?

And then she noticed a window at the end of the corridor, to the left of Marshall's suite. She hurried over to it, slipped its catch and opened it. Sticking her head out, she saw that one of Marshall's windows was open. An exceptionally narrow ledge connected the corridor window to Marshall's. Venus looked at the drop. Although brave, even she would have serious doubts about attempting a stunt like that. Being splattered on the road below wasn't one of her life goals. There had to be an easier way in there. She sighed heavily and hurried back to the lifts.

On her way home from the hotel, Venus got a text.

Sorry V, will b back a bit late, prob 10. Mum x

Venus was reading at the kitchen table when Gail finally came in at ten-fifteen p.m.

'How was your day at the movies?' Gail asked.

'Mum, where have you been?' enquired Venus. 'You said this morning you'd be back well before *nine*.'

'Sorry, honey. My meeting went on far longer than I planned.'

'You've been with them all day?'

Gail nodded. 'One of them is really sharp, but the other's a bit slow.'

'But that's ridiculous, Mum! You've given up the whole of your Saturday to work. It's called the week*end*, remember? It's when you're supposed to slow down and chill out.'

'Don't you get bored sometimes?' asked Gail, changing the conversation, kicking off her shoes and sitting down at the table opposite Venus. 'You know, watching all of these people acting and doing stunts and stuff. Isn't it just painfully slow?'

'No,' replied Venus cautiously, thinking about the madness and noise of the day's army barracks shoot.

'There's always interesting stuff to see. It's not just when the camera's rolling. I like seeing all of the people interact with each other and people bossing each other about.'

'Maybe I should take a day off work some time and hang out with you on one of these sets. It could be fun.'

'Er . . . no, Mum,' replied Venus a little too quickly. 'It's interesting for me because I know loads about it, but it would probably send you to sleep.'

Gail thought about this for a second. 'OK,' she conceded, 'it was just a thought.'

'Sure,' Venus said, smiling with relief. 'Anyway, you're so overloaded with work at the moment that if you took any time off, it should just be for you to relax, unwind.'

Gail nodded slowly. 'You're probably right. I just like to know what you're up to, that's all.'

SUNDAY

The stunt team met at Elstree first thing, because the tech people hadn't got the quarry ready yet for the shoot. Ed Fry had talked to them and shown them a series of photos and diagrams. In a break from his lectures, Venus had made a point of seeking out the Winnebagos. The principal actors and directors all had one to retreat to for a bit of space in the long hours of the shoot. There were ten of them, parked in a line on the far right-hand side of the site. Using the personal delivery ruse again, she'd got a lighting technician to point out which was Scott Marshall's – a large blue one at the far end of the row. Venus made a mental note of it. When the quarry scene was over, she'd come back and check it out.

After a long stretch of waiting around, Ed Fry got the all-clear and the stunt team were driven up to the quarry.

Two hours later, Venus's body and hair were both caked in chalk dust. The stunt team had practised the scene five times and they were ready for a take.

As soon as Ed Fry called 'ACTION!', Venus crawled forwards commando-style, arm over arm, towards the black cross marked on the ground. Her muscles tensed in expectation, awaiting the full force of the blast that was about to rip through the quarry. As the techies fired off the pyrotechnics, two giant wind machines would be activated, literally blowing Venus and her mates backwards towards the edge of the quarry. The machines were so forceful that it took three guys to control each one, and being hurled back by them felt like you'd just suddenly lost touch with gravity.

Venus counted off as she crawled: *Five, four, three . . .*

She was now a metre away from the cross.

Two, one . . .

She screwed up her eyes on cue. The explosion and the wind machines were imminent.

Any second now!

But nothing happened.

No crash; no bang; no rocketing wind.

Venus and the others slowly stood up.

'WHAT THE HELL IS GOING ON?' demanded a furious voice.

Venus spun round. These words weren't spoken by Ed Fry; they came from the mouth of Scott Marshall. Everyone suddenly fell silent and gazed at the director.

'Come on, Scott,' replied Ed Fry, 'it's no big deal. The

explosion didn't fire up. We've already sorted it. We're going again.'

'No, Ed, the problem is NOT sorted!' fumed Marshall. 'You've just cost us thousands of pounds!'

Ed looked at Marshall in disbelief, as if he thought the director might be joking. He was clearly not used to being shouted at in front of the entire second unit and stunt cast.

'I think you're exaggerating slightly, Scott,' pointed out Fry tersely. 'There's no big deal. We're on for take two.'

'EXAGGERATING!' spluttered Marshall. 'We're running HUGE AMOUNTS OVER BUDGET and we can't afford any stupid mistakes like this. There's no margin for error, Ed – I don't want any more of these shoddy mistakes!'

For a second Venus thought that Ed Fry was actually going to hit Marshall, but he regained his cool. Just.

'Listen,' said Fry, lowering his voice, 'we'll talk later. This is the wrong time and place.'

Marshall thought about replying to this, but instead he snorted dismissively and stormed off, leaving a cloud of chalk dust in his wake.

Fry waited till the director was out of sight and then pulled a wry grin. 'That's what you call a seriously overworked guy,' he declared.

Everyone laughed at this tension-busting quip, but Venus could see that Fry was furious with Marshall.

'That was a bit over the top, wasn't it?' asked Venus, walking over to Indigo.

Indigo's top lip curled upwards in contempt. 'Scott Marshall should stick to directing the first unit and leave the stunt scenes to Fry.'

'Does he often turn up on set like that?' asked Venus.

'Yeah,' sneered Indigo harshly. 'When he's not doing one of his own scenes, he likes to stick his nose into other people's business.'

'Right, back to positions, everyone,' Ed Fry declared, breaking up Venus's conversation with Indigo. 'And this time you'll get your explosion,' promised Fry.

There were wry laughs all round, but Venus could see that Fry was still livid about Marshall's verbal onslaught.

Unfortunately, the explosion machine did screw up a second time. Fortunately, Scott Marshall wasn't around to witness it. The third take, however, went like a dream and Fry was delighted with it. Venus had felt the full force of the wind machines and had been thrown about ten metres backwards. She broke her fall smoothly by rolling, and only picked up a couple of bruises.

Venus, Indigo, Brad and Hazel caught the production coach back to Elstree Studios and drank cappuccinos and chatted in a café situated in a small dead-end road next to the studios until the early evening.

'What do you think, Venus? . . .Venus?' Indigo asked.

Venus was miles away. She was busy plotting her next move – Marshall's Winnebago.

'Er . . . yeah, definitely,' agreed Venus, hoping her reply answered whatever the question was.

She looked up at her three companions.

Hazel and Brad were great to hang out with, but Venus thought Indigo was brilliant. Indigo seemed like the kind of person she'd like to be when she was seventeen. She had loads of good stunt stories to tell – her knowledge of the stunt world was phenomenal – but she was also a very good listener. Indigo was going to make it big as a stunt artist – Venus was sure about that. Venus felt like she was learning loads just by being on the same crew as Indigo, studying the cunning ways she did things, like how she broke her falls, positioned herself on steps, or the questions she asked.

At seven-thirty Brad said he had to make a move back to Soho – his brother had just bought some new computer football game and he was itching to try it out. Indigo and Hazel bade their goodnights and headed off home too.

This gave Venus the perfect opportunity. She was just sneaking towards the Winnebago lot, checking her watch, when her mobile suddenly went off.

'Hey, Venus.'

'Jed!'

Venus felt a pang of excitement. Jed had been on holiday in Spain with his family.

'How's it going, Venus?'

'Excellent. Have you just got back?'

'Yeah, only been back five minutes, but I had to phone you. Are you on *AS2* right now?'

'Yeah, it's amazing. I've already done two scenes.'

'No way!'

'It's been brilliant. Yesterday we stormed an army barracks and today we did a quarry explosion!'

'Unreal!' marvelled Jed. 'You deserve it, but I'm *so* envious.'

And damn cute!

'Don't worry, it'll be you soon.'

'You reckon?'

'Definitely.'

'So, are you still on for the weekend after next?' Jed asked.

'Totally! Are you?'

'A hundred per cent. I'll get to my uncle's place by five. He's going to cook for us and then we can hang out. We can give you a lift back home so you don't have to worry about buses or trains.'

'Excellent!' cried Venus. 'Sounds brilliant.'

'When's your next scene?'

'I'm doing a horseback one on Tuesday.'

'That's incredible. But you don't have much experience with horses, do you?'

'No,' said Venus, 'but there was no way I was going to tell anyone here that! It should be simple enough.'

They carried on talking for a while, then Jed had to go. Venus tucked her phone back into her pocket and waited ten minutes, trying to get herself to stop smiling so much and focus on the task at hand. She grabbed her bag and cut back into the studio complex. It was dark now and several of the huge hangars were illuminated against the night sky, looking like the towering banks of football stadiums.

Instead of choosing the path that led towards the front of the studios, Venus took a small path to her left and ended up on a wide stone track. She turned right and about fifty metres down it, took a narrow gravel path. This led directly to the line of Winnebagos.

As she approached Marshall's, she saw there was a light on inside.

That's not so strange. He's obviously a work-round-the-clock kind of guy. But I'll still have a quick peek inside.

She crept forward until she was pressed against the near end of the vehicle. Puffs of wispy smoke were floating out of an open window a couple of metres above her. She could hear a muffled voice inside and she recognised it immediately as Marshall's. She looked around for something to stand on and saw a pile of brown crates, the sort usually used to transport loaves of bread.

Quickly, she tiptoed over, grabbed four of them and hurried back to the side of the Winnebago. Carefully she stacked them on top of each other and then climbed on to her makeshift tower. She raised herself from a crouching position, until her eyes were just level with the bottom of the window.

Marshall was there right in front of her, but fortunately with his back towards her, puffing on a long cigar and talking in a hushed, very aggressive voice on the phone. Unfortunately, she couldn't hear what he was saying. She cursed and scanned the rest of the Winnebago's inside.

It was essentially one big room with a small kitchenette at one end and a bathroom at the other. A large, wooden, rectangular table was pressed against the far wall and there were hundreds of pieces of paper in messy piles stacked up all over its surface. It was impossible to see what was on any of them.

What should I do? Hang around until he's gone and try and break in? Come back tomorrow when he's not around? Call Elliot and Dennis and ask for advice?

But as Venus was trying to figure out a plan, she suddenly heard a sound behind her and spun round.

'Venus?'

It was Indigo.

'What are you doing up there?' hissed Indigo.

Venus felt a rush of relief shoot through her. It would have been so much worse if it was site security.

'I was . . . I was just . . .'

Indigo put a finger on her lips and glanced up quickly at the open Winnebago window. She took Venus by the elbow, helping her down off the crates, and steered her along the path, away from the vehicle.

This short walk gave Venus a chance to compose herself and make up a believable story. 'I was just being nosy,' she said with a weak smile. 'I know it's pathetic, but I'm . . . you know . . . a bit starstruck.'

Indigo took a deep breath. 'It's not worth it, Venus,' she said quietly. 'If someone saw you and grassed on you, you'd be kicked off the picture and might never do stunt work again.'

Venus gulped deeply.

'You're talented and a good laugh,' added Indigo, smiling at Venus. 'I'd hate it if they binned you for doing something stupid like spying on Marshall.'

Venus suddenly felt very small – as if she were an infant and Indigo her nursery teacher. But a thought struck her. 'I thought you went home?'

'I was on my way, but I left this in the canteen,' replied

Indigo, holding up her iPod. 'Come on. Are you going to the bus stop?'

'So at this stage, the only thing we have on Marshall is the fact that he shouted at Ed Fry a bit more harshly than he'd normally shout.'

Dennis Spring was never one to mince his words. He was sitting in his apartment with Elliot and Venus. She'd been briefing them on events so far on *AS2*.

'It's early days,' noted Elliot. 'Venus has only just gone in there. So far she's doing well.'

Venus looked down at the floor as a small thread of pride twisted inside her. This situation was so bizarre; here she was with the father she'd never known and he was praising her and making her blush. If someone had told her a couple of months ago that this would be happening, she'd have laughed in their face.

'So I presume the next stage is to actually get inside Marshall's Winnebago or hotel room?' asked Venus. She'd told them about her initial recces of these two locations.

'Definitely,' replied Elliot. 'Go for the Winnebago. They're famously insecure, whereas hotel rooms are much harder to penetrate.'

Venus nodded. 'And I'm looking for any documents that might show up Marshall cheating the Cribben-Taylors, right?'

'You've got it,' responded Elliot. 'I know it's a long shot, but there *may* be invoices that have been altered, or forged papers or something like that. Anything to do with finances could be useful.'

'Just be careful,' warned Dennis.

'I will be,' Venus assured him.

'OK then,' said Dennis. 'Now we know your next move, does anyone fancy a coffee?'

Venus and Elliot both nodded and watched Dennis disappear into his kitchen.

They sat in silence for a minute.

'So are you going to tell me any more about you and Mum?' Venus eventually asked. 'Or do I just have to keep guessing?'

Venus felt she got to know and trust Elliot a bit more whenever they spent time together, and something within her really wanted to find vital evidence about Marshall that would impress him. However, in spite of these positive emotions, she could also still feel anger burning inside her and she'd accepted that she might always feel that way, whatever story he finally told her. And besides, how long was he going to stay around? Even if she did find something on Scott Marshall, Elliot was bound to disappear back to the States again.

Elliot scratched his cheek and studied his daughter's enquiring face.

'OK, Venus,' he said after a few moments.

She sat up in her chair and fixed her eyes on him.

'I was in London on business,' he began. 'I'd been here for a couple of months and I had an appointment in town.'

Venus nodded and he went on.

'One day, I was passing the College of Law, near the British Museum, and I collided with your mother. It wasn't one of those movie scenes where her papers fluttered through the air and I heroically rescued them. I just literally bumped into her.'

Venus raised an eyebrow as she tried to picture this collision.

'I apologised profusely and was about to go on my way, when something inside urged me to ask if I could buy her a coffee. I stupidly followed my impulse.'

'Why was it stupid?'

Elliot sighed. 'I was involved in . . . all sorts of stuff and making friends wasn't on my agenda, especially not with attractive, female law students.'

'What sort of stuff were you involved with?'

'Government stuff.'

Venus groaned. Talking to Elliot was like talking to a censor – he was always editing out things that she couldn't push him to talk about. 'Well, what did she say?'

'She declined the offer, but I found myself being very insistent and in the end her resolve broke. We headed off to this tiny little Italian café on the corner of the street for cappuccinos. I only had half an hour until my next appointment, but in that short space of time, she totally blew me away. She was amazingly bright, not to mention absolutely gorgeous. She laughed at a couple of my jokes, but I didn't think I'd made any great impact on her. So after getting the bill, I was amazed when she asked for my phone number. Back then, it was usually men who made all the moves, so I realised instantly she was a bold woman, and I liked that. I thought she was just being kind, but a couple of days later, she rang me and asked if I wanted to go to the theatre with some of her friends.'

'And did you?' asked Venus.

Elliot sighed. 'That was the thing – I couldn't. I was too bogged down with work. It was the beginning of a pattern that saw me letting her down repeatedly.'

'So when did you next see her?'

'I almost didn't. I told myself that getting involved with her would be disastrous; there was no way it could work out. But I couldn't help myself. I was really smitten with her. We arranged a dinner date the following week, but I had to cancel that as well.'

'What work was so important?'

'I'll come to that. I finally stuck to a date. I took her out to this really nice country pub one Sunday afternoon; it was funny – me, the American guy, taking this delightful English lady to the most genteel of settings.'

'She fell for it, didn't she?'

Elliot laughed. 'She did, Venus. From then on, I saw her whenever it was possible, which at times wasn't very often, and then . . .'

His words hung in the air.

'And then what?' demanded Venus.

'And then, she told me she was pregnant.'

'With me, right?'

Elliot nodded.

Venus swallowed nervously. 'When did you decide to walk out on us? Was it a spur of the moment decision or had you planned it for ages?'

'I didn't plan to leave you at all! I desperately wanted to stay with her . . . with you . . . but my life was getting very complicated.'

'More complicated than for a young woman with a three-month-old child?' asked Venus, with a steely edge creeping into her voice.

Elliot took a deep breath. 'I know how it looks, Venus, but you've got to believe me – I didn't leave out of choice.'

'Yeah right, just like thousands of other men.'

'No,' Elliot replied softly, 'this wasn't like anyone else. There was a colossal amount at stake in the work part of my life. I had to make the most agonising decision I've ever made. I regret it bitterly to this day, but I couldn't have done it differently.'

At that second, Dennis reappeared with a tray and three cups of coffee. 'Everything OK out here?' he asked, sensing the tension as he put down the tray on a table.

'Everything's fine,' said Elliot, with a nod.

Venus crossed her arms and said nothing.

As Dennis drove Venus home, her mum was sitting at the kitchen table leafing through a huge lever-arch file. Gail's case was going pretty well, but she had another one right after it and at the moment she was feeling like she was on a never-ending rollercoaster.

Forcing herself to switch off from work for a few seconds, she placed the file back on the table and turned her thoughts to Venus. She'd had a distant nagging feeling in the last few months that Venus was probably spending too much time with Dennis on film sets during her school holidays. But on the other hand, wasn't it better that Venus was with her granddad than out on the streets, getting up to whatever mischief teenagers got up to?

Gail knew how much mental and physical time her work took up, but she'd been thinking recently that the heavy demands of her workload meant she was neglecting Venus. It was just that Venus was so mature and confident and could look after herself. In some quiet moments in the evenings, when Gail was working and Venus was out, Gail felt a pang of loss – a yearning for those days when Venus was very young and really needed her. Nowadays they seemed to meet more often than not on the stairs, like two commuters hurrying for different platforms in the morning rush.

Maybe it was time to keep more of an eye on her only daughter. They should hang out together, go out for a meal or something. They could talk and bond. Maybe Gail should book a weekend away – in a health spa or something? Venus was very keen on the gym and swimming, and a trip like that could be a lot of fun.

Gail had just reached for a holiday directory on the shelf when her mobile rang. She checked to see the caller. It was Brian Matheson, one of the barristers on the case. She sighed and replaced the holiday directory on the shelf.

'Brian,' she answered brightly. 'What can I do for you?'

MONDAY

'Are you going to that gig tonight?' asked Indigo.

Some of Brad's mates were in an indie band, and they were performing at the Cube Cellar in East London and he'd asked Venus, Indigo and Hazel to come along.

Indigo and Venus were sitting on some boulders, beside a long, gravel pathway at Elstree Studios. Venus was in a good mood. She'd discovered that Scott Marshall would be off-site all day until about ten p.m.; he had some big scene to direct at the American Embassy. With Marshall out of the way, she'd have a decent opportunity to check out his Winnebago.

'I'm really exhausted so I'd like to give it a miss,' replied Venus. 'But I told my mate Kate about it and she really wants to go.'

Venus picked up a pebble and skimmed it across the ground. The stunt team hadn't been filming that day; they'd been rehearsing. Ed Fry had spent hours going over the next day's horseback scene on Hampstead Heath.

As Jed had reminded her, Venus only had a tiny amount of horse riding experience, but she figured the horses they would be using would be very well-trained and obliging.

'You've done really well on the stunts so far,' remarked Indigo, with an approving nod.

Venus blushed. Praise from Indigo meant something.

They were silent for a few moments.

'So are all of your family in the stunt trade?' enquired Venus.

'My mum and dad met on the set of some rubbish cowboy film,' replied Indigo.

Venus laughed. 'What are they working on now?'

Indigo's face clouded over for a second. 'My mum's retired,' she replied, 'and my dad's dead.'

'Oh God, I'm really sorry,' said Venus softly.

'It's OK, I can deal with it.'

'When . . . when did he die?'

'Ten years ago,' Indigo replied, as she rummaged in her pocket for her ringing mobile and excused herself to take the call. When she returned she told Venus that the caller had been some boy called Jim who really liked her, but she wasn't too keen on him.

Indigo talked about Jim for a while and then asked Venus about her love life. Venus smiled, then gave Indigo the low-down on Jed – how she'd met him at stunt camp, how he was really enthusiastic about the stunt world, gorgeous and totally sweet, and how excited she was that she was finally going to get to spend some time with him soon.

It was past seven-thirty when Indigo said she was collecting her stuff from the rehearsal rooms and going home. Once she'd left, Venus headed straight for the line of Winnebagos, constantly checking over her shoulder to make sure no one was behind her.

She sneaked up to Marshall's Winnebago again. This time the lights were off. She pressed her ear against the side and listened. There was no sound – no tense, muffled phone conversations. Nothing. This was her big chance.

She had it all worked out. She'd noticed that his Winnebago, like many of the others, had a square panel in the roof which doubled up as a kind of window and an emergency exit. She'd brought a couple of screwdrivers with her and was fairly sure she'd be able to prise this hatch open. She could get in and out of there very swiftly.

She glanced at her watch: 8.05.

She checked her surroundings again. There was no sign of anyone.

Venus walked round the back of the Winnebago and hoisted herself up on to a ledge that jutted out from it. From there, she reached up, grabbed a metal rail and pulled herself on to the roof. As soon as she made it, she flattened herself as low as possible on her front and began to snake over to the hatch.

Reaching into her jacket pocket, she withdrew the larger of the two screwdrivers and pushed its edge beneath the rim at the bottom of the hatch to prise it up slightly, allowing her to feel around underneath until she'd located the catch. It was a pretty old vehicle and hadn't been brilliantly looked after. As a result, the seal round the hatch was fairly loose and she smiled to herself as she began to prise it open.

She took it in her hands and levered it up and silently flipped it over on to the roof's surface. She scanned her surroundings again. She was alone. She then listened carefully just in case Marshall had blown out his meeting and was in there asleep in the dark. But she couldn't detect the slightest sound or even the faintest whisper of breath.

Slowly, she lowered herself through the hatch opening and landed with a quiet thud on the floor of the Winnebago. Her skin prickled with nerves. This was her chance to have a proper root around and hopefully get something on Scott Marshall.

She switched on her torch. In front of her was the paper-strewn table she'd seen the previous night. She picked up a document. It was a script. She thumbed through it, and various other documents. There were pages and pages of scripts covered in scribbles. There was no computer in the Winnebago. Getting to Marshall's computer could prove very handy, but it wasn't going to happen that night.

Everything was completely unrelated to finances – it was all scripts – and she suddenly felt very downhearted. She'd gone to all of this trouble and had made zero progress.

But at that second she suddenly heard the hatch thud shut. Her heart leaped in shock. She spun round to glimpse a figure bringing a raised, heavy-looking object down towards her.

The last thing she remembered was falling to the ground.

When Venus came round, she was lying face-down on the floor of Marshall's Winnebago. Her head was throbbing badly and she felt around her scalp to see if there was any blood. There wasn't, but a bump was already beginning to protrude.

She checked her watch: 8.17. She could have only been out for a couple of minutes.

Groggily, she raised her head, but it felt like a lead weight and she sank back down to the floor. She tried again, this time lifting it centimetre by centimetre. She looked around her and spotted that the Winnebago door was open. It had been closed when she arrived a few minutes ago.

Marshall must have come back early from his shoot, seen her climb up on the roof and sneak inside, waited for her to drop in and then whacked her on the back of her head.

He either thought I was a burglar and wanted to surprise me or he has something to hide. Either way, he might have alerted security. He could be on his way back here with them at this very second.

These thoughts made Venus panic – if she was caught she might never work in the stunt world again.

Venus dragged herself to her feet and staggered shakily out of the door. She nearly fell as her feet hit the path outside and she had to lean against the side of the Winnebago for a few seconds. But there was no sign of Scott Marshall and an army of security guards.

It took her ten minutes to make it to the canteen. A woman was scrubbing down tables and a lone man was listening to an MP3 player with his eyes closed.

Venus approached the woman.

'Can I ask you a favour?' she began.

'What is it, love?' asked the woman.

'Er . . . have you got any ice?'

'What, for drinks?'

'No . . . for . . . my head.'

The woman looked puzzled. 'Have you taken a hit there?'

Venus nodded.

'Well, you should go straight to medical, they'll sort you out.'

Venus smiled weakly. 'It didn't happen on a shoot . . . it . . . er . . . it happened when I was messing about . . . on . . . on . . . someone's skateboard.'

The woman looked her up and down. 'All right, I'll get you some ice, but you should be more careful – some of those skateboard tricks are lethal. And I still reckon you should get medical to check you over. You look very pale.'

'I'll be fine in a minute,' replied Venus.

The woman looked at her doubtfully and disappeared into the back of the canteen. She returned a minute later with a large pack of ice wrapped in a cloth.

'Thanks,' Venus said gratefully, as she took the pack. 'I really appreciate this.'

'That's OK, love.' The woman smiled. 'Just take a bit more care of yourself.'

Venus thanked her again and slipped out of the canteen. She walked about thirty metres, then collapsed on to a nearby bench and pressed the ice against her head. It instantly offered some pain relief.

She picked up her phone to text Elliot and Dennis, but was uncertain what she should say. In the end, she decided to tell them there was nothing of use in the Winnebago, but not to let them know about the attack; they'd only freak out and they might even pull her out of the investigation, and Venus wanted the chance to prove herself to both Dennis and Elliot.

As Venus sent the text, her text alert bleeped.

Am about 2 go on tube. C u @ the gig. Kate x

Venus cursed. She'd forgotten to tell Kate she wasn't going, and Kate would be out of reception for the whole tube journey. And however bad she felt, she couldn't let Kate turn up at the Cube Cellar by herself, not knowing anyone.

There was only one thing for it.

As Venus walked through the Cube Cellar, she spied Indigo at the far side of the room, chatting to Brad and Hazel. Kate was sitting by herself at the bar, sipping mineral water. She tapped Kate on the shoulder and took her over to meet her stunt mates.

'It's great to see you!' Indigo exclaimed. 'I reckoned you might give tonight a miss – I thought you were exhausted.'

Venus touched the back of her head gingerly. 'I am,' she said, 'but a gig is a gig!'

There were at least a hundred people down there and the place was filled with music, voices and laughter. Indigo went off to the loo, so Venus and Hazel began chatting and Brad latched on to Kate. Venus smiled at this. She could instantly see that Brad was pretty taken with Kate; loads of boys were. She wasn't only attractive, she was approachable as well and guys loved that. However,

Venus could also see from Kate's closed body language and doing-her-best-to-look-interested expression that she wasn't keen on Brad in *that* way.

'Are you OK?' asked Indigo, returning.

'Yeah, why shouldn't I be?' replied Venus, a tad too quickly for her own liking.

'It's just . . . you seem kind of quiet tonight,' replied Indigo, looking at the back of Venus's head.

Oh my God, she's seen the bump on my head! She's going to ask how I got it!

But Indigo said nothing.

'I'm cool,' replied Venus, twisting slightly so the bump would be out of Indigo's sight.

'Good,' said Indigo with a smile.

'Can I get you ladies another drink?' offered Brad.

'That's extremely chivalrous of you,' Kate said, smiling as Venus and Indigo also accepted his offer.

As Brad went off to get the drinks, the band came on. They were four Aussie guys, real Brad-types. Their music was full of jangly guitars and amp distortions – the kind of music Venus detested, but she did her best to join Kate and Indigo in dancing and applauding the band.

'They're brilliant, aren't they?' shouted Brad, when they'd done their final encore.

Venus nodded slowly, keen not to give her head any more shocks tonight.

Brad was staying on to hang out with the band and Indigo had decided to join him.

'Do you two want to come?' asked Brad, looking hopefully at Kate.

'Not me,' replied Venus, 'though you can, Kate.'

'Er, no thanks,' said Kate, 'I'm tired.'

'Will I see you again?' asked Brad, looking at Kate.

'That would be good,' replied Kate tactfully.

As Venus and Kate headed for the cloakroom, Venus flicked Kate on the shoulder. 'I think Brad kind of liked you,' she said.

'Possibly,' said Kate, grinning. 'He's a sweet guy, but so not my type.'

Venus nodded. 'He looked a bit crushed,' she observed.

'I'm sure he gets plenty of girls,' said Kate. 'Anyway, I'm going to the loo. Coming?'

'Nah,' replied Venus, 'I'll see you in a second.'

Venus pulled on her jacket and tapped her feet on the floor, humming a tune she'd heard on a radio back at Elstree Studios earlier in the evening. After a minute or so, the surly woman in the cloakroom disappeared somewhere, exposing a set of three CCTV monitors.

Venus's eyes had just drifted towards them when she suddenly felt a stabbing pain in the centre of her chest.

On the central TV monitor, a face stared out at her. It looked just like Franco.

The tap on Venus's shoulder made her jump in terror.

'Hey, Venus,' said Kate, 'what's going on?'

Venus felt her body shake as she pointed to the TV screens.

'What is it?' asked a bewildered Kate.

Venus turned back to the monitors. The face had gone.

'Are you absolutely sure it was him?' asked Kate, after Venus explained what had happened.

Venus shook her head grimly. 'I don't know . . . I'm not sure . . . Maybe I imagined it.'

Venus then told Kate all about the incident in the Winnebago.

'You got hit on the head, yet you still came tonight?' asked Kate.

Venus nodded.

'Venus!' exclaimed Kate. 'What am I going to do with you?'

Venus managed a weak smile.

'It would definitely explain why you might be seeing things,' Kate pointed out. 'Shouldn't you go to hospital?'

Venus gingerly shook her head. 'No, it's fine. And you're probably right – I probably am seeing things.'

Kate threaded her arm through Venus's. 'Let's go home,' she said.

As they walked off down the street, Venus felt the tensions of the day wash over her: the whack on her head, the face on the screen. Could it have been Franco? She hoped to God it wasn't – her life was complicated enough right now without him turning up.

TUESDAY

The sun filtered down through the branches of the giant oak trees, creating long, thin shadows that danced across the lush green grass. The sky was a tranquil blue. It was seven-thirty a.m. – a beautiful October morning on London's Hampstead Heath.

The car had come for Venus at five-thirty and she made it to the location by six, just as Ed Fry had instructed. This had involved a five a.m. alarm call, which had nearly killed her. She'd told her mum the night before about the early start.

In the car, Venus's mind zipped over the events of the previous day: Marshall hitting her in his Winnebago; seeing Franco – or a very close Franco lookalike – on the screen at the Cube Cellar. It felt like events were getting a bit out of control and she made a firm resolution to remain calm, if possible.

Anyway, it probably hadn't been Franco, and as for Scott Marshall, well he hadn't seen her on set, and so he wouldn't have recognised her; she'd just have to be on her guard.

The members of the *AS2* second unit had worked through the night setting up the horse shoot and several of them looked seriously worse for wear. They'd taken over a huge oval of ground, right in the middle of the Heath. The entire area had been marked with crosses and lines for the stunt artists to use to guide them, but that would be out of shot. What would appear on cinema screens as a spontaneous, fast-paced, thirty-second chase, had taken hours to set up and a whole army of people to facilitate.

They'd erected a huge stretch of metal barriers round the space. A string of security guards were standing at various strategic points, just in case a zealous member of the public tried to get a closer look at the bizarre 'circus' that had sprung up during the night.

Venus had been on horseback twice; once on a pony on the set of *The Power of the Wind*, and a short session during Dennis's summer stunt camp. She had confided in Indigo that she had little experience in handling horses, but she certainly wasn't going to mention this to Ed Fry when he'd asked her if she was up for a horse stunt.

Indigo was already there when Venus arrived, as were Brad and Hazel, who'd already filmed a horse-free scene. Indigo told Venus all about the horses they'd be riding.

'They're called Kyle and Prince,' Indigo explained, 'and I've tried them both out. Prince seems by far the easier, so I'll let you ride him.'

Venus breathed a deep sigh of relief. It was good of Indigo to make things easier for her.

Kyle was a black horse with a long white stripe down his forehead. Prince was a gorgeous chestnut, strong and sleek. There was a team of four hands from Kyle and Prince's stables who attended to their needs in minute detail. There was also a guy from a central animal casting unit who was on hand to ensure that both horses were treated humanely. The head of the horse team was a woman called Jan, who was rather stereotypically wearing a Barbour jacket and an Alice band.

'Prince can be a problem but I've heard you're an experienced rider,' Jan told Venus. Venus swallowed nervously as Jan chatted to her about handling the horses, then gave her a leg up on to Prince's back. She'd been really up for this scene when she first heard about it, but now looking at the two giant horses in front of her, she couldn't help wishing someone else had been selected.

Venus trotted and cantered round the space. After half an hour with Prince, she felt like she'd got to know him and was a bit more confident.

When she dismounted, she spotted Ed Fry addressing a large group of the production team, pointing at a series of storyboards for the umpteenth time – determined to get every tiny detail right.

The scene opened with a bout of hand-to-hand combat. Venus and Indigo would fight a group of villains, manage to break away, mount horses and ride to freedom. The baddies had currently congregated under a tree. They were wearing combat gear, sipping tea in polystyrene cups and sharing jokes.

'All set?' asked Indigo, walking over to Venus.

'Sure,' replied Venus, not feeling that sure at all. She stroked Prince's neck and looked over her shoulder to see where Ed Fry was. He was now issuing instructions to a couple of runners. Venus rubbed her clammy hands together. This was easily the most demanding stunt she'd ever faced.

Fry finished with the runners and sent the baddies over to their starting point under the huge tree. The horse people were attending to Prince and Kyle and giving them a last-minute brush down.

'Are you two OK?' Fry called over to Venus and Indigo. They gave him the thumbs up.

A couple of members of the public had shown up and were watching expectantly. The guards were speaking to them, presumably stressing the importance of their being silent when the cameras were rolling.

Ed Fry waved his arm in the air at Venus and Indigo.

'We're on!' he shouted.

Venus and Indigo walked over towards their enemies – four guys and two women. Venus had only met them the previous day for a couple of hours and briefly thought it was odd she'd spent most of that time fighting them!

Venus and Indigo lined up in their positions. The first section of the scene was being filmed by two cameras – one hoisted up on a tall crane unit, the other mounted on a track along the ground.

Two floor managers shouted out several times for quiet.

The second the word 'ACTION!' was out of Ed Fry's mouth, Venus hit out. She caught one of the female baddies with a fake blow to the stomach. The woman doubled over, then hit back, but Venus parried the blow with her right arm, swinging round and seemingly high-kicking her enemy to the ground.

Instantly, one of the men lunged at her. Venus exchanged blows with this new opponent and then pushed him with all of her strength. He cried out in shock and tumbled backwards.

If all was going to plan, this was the second when Indigo made her break, with Venus close behind. And sure enough, Indigo, having fought off two of the enemy guys, sprinted to the left. Venus flew after her. Prince and Kyle were tethered to a wooden post about twenty metres ahead.

Venus grabbed at the rope tied to Prince, threw it off the post, and sprung on to his back. Indigo did exactly the same with Kyle.

The furious footsteps of the baddies sounded behind them, but within seven seconds, Venus and Indigo were off. Venus held tightly on to Prince's reins as he thundered forward. She felt elation as he pounded ahead and the cool morning air brushed her cheeks. It had felt good to race him earlier, but now he was really flying.

This is fantastic!

Prince and Kyle thundered on, side by side – two majestic beasts speeding in the hazy light. The cries of the villains behind them grew fainter as the horses pulled away and a few seconds later, Fry called out a very satisfied, 'CUT!'

Indigo dismounted Kyle and handed his reins over to Jan, but Venus had so enjoyed the stunt that she wanted to stay on Prince for a bit longer. She trotted in a circle for a few minutes. She was about to begin the short canter back to the crew and the horse team, when a car horn screeched out through the morning air.

Jan pulled Kyle's reins and he calmed down.

But Prince bolted.

By the time Venus realised what was happening, it was too late to contain him. The noise had completely freaked him out and he was very eager to get as far away from it as possible.

'HEY, PRINCE!' shouted Venus, struggling just to keep hold of his reins and stay upright. The horse thundered across the grass, gaining speed all the time, his powerful hooves crunching down on the ground. To her horror, Venus saw that he was heading straight for a long metal barrier.

'NO, PRINCE!' she yelled, pulling the reins as the wind whipped her face while he continued to pick up speed, snorting wildly in distress.

None of Venus's minuscule equestrian experience was of any use now. On he flew and, just in front of the barrier, Prince's hooves left the ground.

'NOOOO!' shrieked Venus, clutching his neck tightly and seeing the small throng of people part as Prince crashed right over the fence. He galloped on, shaking his head wildly. Through another field he charged, nearly mowing down two businessmen in suits.

'STOP, PRINCE! STOP!' shouted Venus, but he was in no mood for halting. As he sprinted on, Venus managed to turn his head slightly and guide him towards some woodland. He slowed slightly as he neared the trees, but showed no signs of stopping. With this in mind, she falteringly stood up in the stirrups and pulled her left leg over Prince's back, so she was standing just in her right stirrup. They whipped past a clump of trees, Prince's hooves stamping over the bed of leaves on the ground.

Venus saw the tree a couple of seconds before jumping. As it came into view, she spied the branch. It was at a perfect height. Without giving it any more thought, she propelled herself off the horse. As her body spun through the air, she reached out and grabbed at the branch. She swung a couple of times and then her body straightened out and she let herself fall to the ground. She rolled over to break her fall, thankful that she'd escaped without suffering any serious injury.

She looked around her, but Prince was already out of sight. Venus thought about following him, but she'd never get anywhere near him. She just hoped he would calm down quickly, before something happened either to him or to someone who happened to be standing in his way.

Venus started crossing the woodland, selecting what she reckoned was a more direct route back to the set than the one she and Prince had taken. She was nearing the edge of the woodland when she spotted a figure up ahead of her, standing side-on beside a bench.

It was Scott Marshall.

Instinctively, Venus pulled back behind a tree. Marshall was on his mobile and to say he appeared agitated was an understatement. His expression was anguished, his forehead was covered in beads of sweat and he was pacing around anxiously.

Taking a couple of steps forward, Venus darted behind

another tree. She had just taken another four steps, when Marshall spun round. Luckily, Venus had moved quicker than him and was shielded again from his view behind a tree.

Another five steps later and she could hear some of what he was saying.

'Get the money sorted immediately.'

Venus's eyes widened and she moved forward again.

The person on the other end of the phone was clearly not completely compliant with Marshall's instructions, because the *AS2* director hissed into his phone furiously. *'I said get the money sorted now or you and I are heading straight for prison. Do you get me?'*

A second later, the phonecall was over.

Venus hung back and watched Marshall pocket his phone and head directly towards her. Her heart dive-bombed.

He must have seen me! And if he recognises me from his Winnebago, he's not going to take too kindly to me spying on him now!

She waited for Marshall to reach her and to launch into a verbal onslaught, but instead, he walked straight past her.

He hadn't spotted her. By the thunderous look on his face, he had more pressing matters to deal with.

Venus waited a couple of minutes before she headed back to the set, her mind still going over Marshall's phone conversation. Surely this was proof of his wrongdoing? The phone record on his mobile could show whom the call was with; maybe it could link Marshall to whoever was in it with him? As she got closer, Ed Fry and Indigo sped over to her.

'Are you all right?' shouted a very concerned-looking Fry. 'I know you're an experienced rider, but still . . .'

'I . . . I . . . am,' replied Venus, trying to keep her voice calm. 'I'm fine – it's no big deal. Where's Prince?'

'He's back with the horse team,' said Fry. 'He just got a terrible fright.'

'And barely a scratch on you,' marvelled Indigo.

Venus laughed nervously. 'Lucky break!' she replied. 'I jumped off and caught a branch before I got scythed.'

A camera guy called Fry away, and Venus and Indigo headed over to the tea van for some much needed refreshment.

'I can't believe Prince bolted,' mused Venus, as she gulped her tea. 'I mean the whole stunt set-up thing feels pretty safe. Ed Fry seems to have it all under control – what idiot would use a car horn with horses around? I could have been seriously hurt.'

'Stuff happens on films,' replied Indigo, her face suddenly looking stern. 'If the right checks and balances aren't in place . . . things can get nasty.'

Venus was about to reply to this, but Indigo was called

by one of the tech team to help them.

On her return home, Venus crashed out and slept for ages. She woke up mid-afternoon, grabbed some toast and went back to bed. When she finally emerged at six-thirty p.m. she had a long soak in the bath and went over the words she'd heard Marshall saying that morning on the Heath.

'. . . *get the money sorted now or you and I are heading straight for prison. Do you get me?*'

She was on to him – she knew she was. It was time to move on to the next stage of her investigation.

WEDNESDAY

It was ten a.m. by the time Venus approached the security hut at the front of Elstree Studios. She'd briefed Elliot and Dennis the night before about the overheard Scott Marshall conversation. They both agreed with her – it certainly seemed as if Marshall was up to something. She flashed her pass, but to her surprise, when the guard read her name, he motioned for her to wait a moment.

He reached over to a table just behind him and handed over a brown envelope with her name typed on the front. She walked a few metres away from the hut and opened it. Inside was a piece of white paper with two words, written in thick black ink.

BACK OFF

Venus felt a shiver tingle down her spine.

OK, if it had been Marshall who had whacked her on the head – and she was pretty sure it was – this meant he must know who she was.

But if he's worried that I'm on to him, why doesn't he just fire me and send me well away from him? Why is he just warning me off? Maybe he doesn't want to draw attention to himself and thinks I'll just crumble when I see this note and flee . . . Well, if he thinks that, he's wrong.

She hurried back to the security hut. The guard stared out at her.

'Excuse me,' she asked, waving the envelope, 'do you know who handed this letter in?'

The guard shook his head. 'Someone posted it under the door,' he replied. 'It was here when I came in this morning. Why? Is anything wrong?'

Venus shook her head. 'No,' she replied, 'everything's fine.'

Hangar 17 was vast and was teeming with activity. An enormous tank of water stood in the centre of the hangar, with a replica tail-end of a giant ship in the middle. There were people swarming all over the deck, like ants in a sugar bowl. Painters were touching up the bodywork, electricians were concealing wires, carpenters were sawing and sanding. Venus took a deep breath to steady herself. This was going to be the mother of all scenes.

It involved Indigo and Venus commandeering a ship that was on the verge of sinking. Through their skill and abilities, they would save the ship and capture their terrifying nemesis.

The scene opened with Indigo battling two warriors at the front of the ship, while Venus ran to help her. But as Venus sped down the deck, the ship would hit a massive wave and water would cascade down on to Venus, knocking her overboard. She'd ride the wave, swim to the front and join Indigo for the fight.

Venus stared up at the eight giant water tanks above the ship's deck. Four of them would be tipped down on to her – controlled by computer. She gulped nervously. That was a serious amount of water.

But Venus didn't have long to dwell on this.

'OK, we're on!' shouted Ed Fry.

Venus climbed over a railing and stood on the deck.

'Where's Indigo?' yelled Fry.

Right on cue, Indigo appeared. 'Sorry,' she said.

Fry checked his watch irritably. 'OK, let's get going.'

Venus was buzzing with adrenaline. The moment Fry shouted 'ACTION!' she was out of her starting position and haring down the deck. Thanks to Fry's in-depth brief of how this scene panned out, she was completely ready for the sound of the water unleashing on top of her.

The second her right foot hit the mark, the tanks were released, instantly submerging her in an avalanche of water and sweeping her into the immense main tank. Her body was dragged forward and down and she let herself go with it, exactly as Ed had told her.

She counted off in her head.

One, two, three, four, five . . .

On fifteen seconds, a current would be generated to help her emerge from the water and she'd swim towards the safety of a lifeboat.

Six, seven, eight, nine, ten . . .

Five more seconds and she'd rise above the water.

Eleven, twelve . . .

She tensed her muscles, preparing for the uplift and the tough swim to safety.

Thirteen, fourteen.

Here it comes!

Fifteen!

She was perfectly ready for the uplift, but to her horror, it didn't happen. Instead she felt her body plunge *lower* into the water.

Her mind raced as she was pushed further down.

What the hell . . . ?

Still her body sank.

This isn't right.

She pushed out her arms to propel herself up and out of this soaking vortex, but she didn't stand a chance. The spiralling current was far too powerful and it dragged her further and further into its centre.

Oh my God! Something's gone wrong!

Again she tried to pull and kick against the water to

rise, but the seemingly unending torrent wouldn't let her. At least forty seconds must have passed now and her chest and lungs were beginning to feel the strain.

Panic began to set in.

I can hold my breath for a minute and a half under water, but after that I'm in drowning territory.

As this thought flashed through her mind, she began furiously to beat her arms against the water to get some, any, leverage against the ferocious current, but she'd been under the water for more than a minute. She couldn't last much longer.

What a horrific way to die!

Her arms were getting weak from trying to propel herself to freedom, her chest was now aching badly, her mind filled with dark thoughts.

I'm never going to see Mum again or Elliot or Dennis or Kate . . . or Jed.

Focusing all of her strength in her legs, she made one last desperate attempt. She kicked down wildly and suddenly felt her body shooting up out of the water. She fell back to the surface and flew forward towards a rail. She reached out frantically and grabbed hold of it, taking massive gulps of breath as the vast waves subsided.

She heard a cacophony of screaming voices and the noise of feet running.

Indigo made it to her first, her face white with horror.

'I can't believe this has happened! Venus! Venus! It's Indigo! Are you OK? Talk to me! Talk to me!'

Venus took a giant gasp of breath and coughed up another lungful of water.

Indigo shook her by the shoulders. 'Come on, Venus! Say something!'

'I'm OK,' Venus whispered hoarsely, 'but I'd be better if you didn't shake me.'

'Oh my God, sorry,' said Indigo, abruptly letting go.

Venus managed a weak smile. A few seconds later, Venus heard another female voice, but this one was very calm.

'I'm Alice,' said a woman, appearing next to Indigo and wrapping a huge towel round Venus's shoulders. 'I'm a paramedic. In a minute we're going to check you over. You're going to be fine, though. Don't talk, just conserve your energy.'

'Is she going to be OK?' demanded Indigo shakily.

Alice nodded. 'She'll be fine, she just needs to rest.'

At that moment Ed Fry turned up, his face covered in sweat and anxiety.

'Venus, are you OK?' he asked urgently.

'She's going to be fine,' replied Alice.

'Did I screw up, Ed?' asked Venus quietly.

Fry shook his head. 'Not at all. What happened was that

instead of four water tanks opening, all eight of them did. You were incredibly lucky not to drown. But you were also brilliant and we can use the footage in the film.'

'Let's not talk about that right this second,' said Alice firmly. 'I want to check Venus over, so I need you two to leave us for a few minutes.'

Indigo and Fry nodded, gave Venus a last look and then disappeared.

Venus spluttered out some more water as the whole incident came back to her.

Instead of four water tanks opening, all eight of them did.

A chilling thought suddenly struck her.

Marshall! He must be behind this. It makes complete sense. First he attacked me in his Winnebago, then he warned me off and now he tried to drown me. This is edging into terrifying territory.

Venus made an attempt to sit up, but Alice motioned for her not to.

'You swallowed quite a lot of water,' Alice explained, 'but you're obviously a very strong swimmer, because you managed to rise above an unbelievably powerful current.'

Venus closed her eyes and let her breathing slowly calm down.

Alice took Venus's pulse, listened to her heartbeat and checked her blood pressure, eventually satisfied that Venus hadn't suffered any lasting damage.

Ten minutes later, Alice helped Venus very slowly to stand up.

'Is Scott Marshall around?' asked Venus weakly.

'Don't worry about Scott Marshall now,' Alice tutted, 'let's just get you back on your feet.'

Venus's legs felt wobbly and, for a second, she was sure they were going to buckle from the strain and cause her to fall over in a dramatic faint. But she steadied herself and started taking small footsteps, with Alice holding her elbow for support. A couple of minutes later, they reached an ambulance. The tailgate was down and they sat on it together.

'We're going to keep an eye on you for the next hour,' explained Alice, 'and if all is well, we're getting you straight into a cab and sending you home. Is there someone you want to call, like your mum . . . ?'

'No,' replied Venus sharply, 'I'll be fine.'

Alice frowned. 'Don't you get on?' she asked.

'It's not that,' she explained. 'She's just got a lot of work pressure on her at the minute and seeing as I'm OK, I don't want to freak her out.'

Alice thought about this for a few seconds. 'If that's the way you want it, then fine. I'll walk you over to the canteen. We'll get a hot drink inside you and get you home. Thankfully the scene is a wrap so you don't have to go near water again while you're here.'

An hour later, with Venus feeling much better, Alice ushered her into one of the production cars in front of the studio main gates.

The female cabbie who drove Venus home was a veteran studio driver. 'They said there was a bit of an accident today in the tank,' she said conversationally.

'That's right,' yawned Venus.

'Glad you're all right. I've heard of a good few accidents over the years. I remember driving some people home after that terrible accident at Oakley Studios. Do you remember it? *Beast Survival*? The one with Saffron Ritchie?'

Venus wearily shook her head. 'That movie came out when I was little.'

"Course you were,' replied the driver. 'It was a terrible business that – an exploding lighting rig – three people dead. Scott Marshall was the producer. Mind you, he wasn't as famous back then.'

The driver went on talking, but Venus's eyelids felt like lead weights and the pull of sleep was too overpowering. Her eyes shut and a few seconds later, she was out. She woke when the car pulled up outside Dennis's place.

Dennis was waiting by the front door, his face taut with worry. He opened the car door and helped Venus out. He thanked the driver as she turned her car round and headed back to Elstree.

Dennis led Venus inside and shut the front door. He then

gave her an enormous hug. He let her go and fixed his eyes on her. 'Ed Fry told me what happened. He said a computer error was responsible for opening those tanks, but the computer team insist they'd triple checked the calculations.'

Venus winced and pushed the palm of her right hand against her aching chest.

'Do you think Scott Marshall is so terrified of me finding out about his money scam that he'd *kill* me to keep it a secret?'

Dennis pursed his lips anxiously. 'I don't know, Venus – he's an extremely resourceful and determined guy. If he is up to something he might want to prevent people exposing him at all costs. He could have rigged the computer.'

He paused for a second and stared into Venus's eyes. 'Either way, though, I'm pulling you out of there. It's become too dangerous.'

'But there's one stunt left!' Venus protested, with a cough. 'It's just a jump scene. It will look really rubbish if I pull out now. I could get a bad name in the industry.'

'Don't be ridiculous!' Dennis thundered. 'You're only fourteen. You've got your whole career ahead of you. You don't need to worry about your reputation quite yet. And it would be totally understandable to be shaken after an accident like this.'

Venus felt a tide of frustration sweeping over her. 'Please, Granddad. We still haven't got a single shred of evidence that Marshall *is* caught up with something. I'm going to investigate his hotel room tomorrow, as we planned.'

Dennis blew out his cheeks. 'I'm going to get to the bottom of this and see if it *was* an accident.'

'Fine,' Venus agreed, 'but if it *was* an accident, I get to do the final stunt.'

'We'll see,' replied Dennis.

Venus had made it only to the bottom of Dennis's road when she spotted Elliot getting off a bus.

'Hey, Venus,' he said, breaking into a grin, 'are you on your way to Dennis's place?'

Venus shook her head. 'It's been a bit of a mad day and Dennis has commanded me to go home and get some sleep.'

'What's been mad?'

'I'll fill you in.'

Five minutes later, the two of them were sitting on a park bench with a takeaway coffee each. It took Venus fifteen minutes to regale Elliot with the day's drama. Elliot was shocked and became quite agitated when she described her fight to stop drowning.

'My God, Venus,' he muttered, 'you could have been killed!'

'I've made an agreement with Dennis,' said Venus. 'If

the computer system was tampered with, I'm out of there. If there's no proof of it, I do my last stunt on Friday.'

Elliot sighed wearily and rubbed his eyes. 'This is all my fault,' he murmured. 'I should never have allowed you to go in there. I don't see you since you're three months old and when I do finally meet up with you, I agree to you doing my job for me and nearly getting drowned in the process. Talk about being a terrible father.'

They sat in silence for a few moments, sipping their coffees. Venus kicked a pebble over the ground. She'd got used to spending time with Elliot and realised that her anger towards him was gradually ebbing away.

'Come on then,' she suddenly urged, 'I want to hear more about what happened after the break-up with Mum.'

Elliot took a sip of his coffee. 'The period after you were born was incredible,' he began. 'You were the best thing that had ever happened to either of us.'

'But something went wrong, yeah?'

Elliot nodded. 'I've told you; I was leading this other life and things in that world were really kicking off.'

'Why couldn't you just close the door to it?'

'It wasn't like that. The demands that were being placed on me by this other world were dragging me further and further away from you and your mother. I would have given anything to change this, but it wasn't possible.'

'Did you tell her what was going on? Did you warn her?'

Elliot grimaced. 'I couldn't, Venus, I really couldn't. Things were getting . . . dangerous.'

'How?'

Elliot sighed. 'Let's just say that when things exploded, I had to get out of the country as quickly as possible.'

'Were the police after you?'

'No, I just had to get out, or else . . .'

'Or else what?'

'Or else, there'd be a lot of trouble,' said Elliot. 'So that's what I did. I fled. And I couldn't tell *anyone*. But I was a hundred per cent committed to getting back to you and Gail as soon as things had cooled down.'

'So what went wrong?' demanded Venus.

'The cooling-down period took longer than I thought. I figured on a couple of weeks, but in the end it was six. The minute I could, I contacted Gail to explain. But she wasn't having it.'

'Maybe you didn't try hard enough,' said Venus.

'I did,' replied Elliot. 'I did absolutely everything. But Gail wouldn't listen to me – to the truth.'

'You can understand why, can't you?' pointed out Venus. 'She probably thought you were a criminal or something.'

Elliot nodded. 'She did,' he replied. 'She thought I was

bad news. She completely refused to speak to me.'

'So what did you do?'

'I flew straight over here and tried to see her, but it was impossible. She'd made up her mind to cut me out of her life and that was that.'

'Did you keep trying?'

'Yes! Loads of times, but nothing I did made any difference. After a year, I gave up. I was mortified. I'd been told I could never see my partner or child again and I didn't have a legal leg to stand on. I'd walked out on her and no court would ever grant me access to you. Dennis tried to persuade Gail, but she wouldn't be swayed.'

They sat in silence for a few minutes.

'Hearing this from you makes me see everything differently,' murmured Venus. 'I mean, I don't know what to think any more.'

Elliot gave her a sympathetic smile. 'I understand,' he said, 'there's a lot to take in.'

When Venus got home, the house was empty. She spoke to Jed briefly. Talking to him always took her mind off any trouble in her life – at least for a few minutes.

She'd just gone into the kitchen and grabbed a Coke from the fridge when her mobile bleeped.

Working late, hon – sorry. How bout u + me go out 2 supper 1 nite nxt week? It would b good 2 catch up. Mum x

Venus sighed. It would be great to go out, but her mum was working ridiculously hard at the minute. Gail needed to put the brakes on a bit or she'd burn herself out. As Venus thought this, she suddenly realised that she sounded like the parent and Gail like the child. She'd have to mention this in their 'catching-up' session.

Venus felt a wave of exhaustion sweep over her. She grabbed a newspaper off the kitchen table, but only managed to read a couple of paragraphs before she crashed out.

THURSDAY

An hour after Gail left for work the next morning, the doorbell rang. Venus pulled back the curtain and looked out of the window.

It was Dennis.

He came in and sat down at the kitchen table, declining her offer of a drink. Venus sat down opposite him.

'OK,' he began, 'this is the situation.'

Venus eyed him expectantly.

'It definitely was a computer error, either caused by a malfunction on the hard drive or by someone inputting some dodgy data. The tech guys swear none of them did a bad input.'

'Well, they would say that, wouldn't they?' pointed out Venus.

Dennis shook his head. 'Each of their sessions is recorded. It wasn't them.'

'So it was a malfunction or Marshall did it,' Venus said.

'It couldn't have been Marshall,' replied Dennis,

'because he was ten miles away checking out some last-minute details at an old postal depot. They're filming there tomorrow.'

'Maybe he messed with the computer earlier?'

Dennis shook his head. 'I told you; the tech guys have definitive proof of the time the error occurred. There's absolutely no way Marshall could have done it.'

'It could have been someone working for him,' Venus suggested.

Dennis scratched his cheek. 'It's a possibility . . .'

'So can I stay on the set?' asked Venus, hopeful of being able to complete her last stunt.

Dennis took a very deep breath. 'Yes,' he responded, 'but you must be extra vigilant.'

'It could just have been a computer malfunction,' Venus said, trying to reassure him.

'These things happen,' mused Dennis. 'From time to time, horrendous accidents do occur.'

'Yeah, I know. That taxi driver was telling me about some accident on the set of a film years ago, when a lighting rig exploded.'

Dennis nodded. '*Beast Survival.* I remember it well. Two excellent tech people and a brilliant stunt guy called Dave Forrest died.' Venus was about to ask Dennis some questions about *Beast Survival*, but her mobile went and the name Jed flashed up. She excused herself and left the room. Some phonecalls just *had* to be taken.

Venus arrived at the Pine Lodge Hotel, just after ten a.m. She'd found nothing in Scott Marshall's Winnebago – she'd managed to have a pretty thorough search before she was attacked.

That left his hotel room.

She'd heard that he wouldn't be returning to the hotel until after lunch. That gave her loads of time and was the perfect opportunity for her plan.

Walking in through the revolving doors, she made a beeline for the lift. At the fourth floor, she scouted round for the inevitable cleaning lady. Down one of the corridors, she finally saw a woman pushing a high cleaning trolley further down. Venus strode in her direction.

'Hi,' Venus said, smiling and flashing her Elstree security pass. 'I'm a production assistant on *Airborne Sword 2*. Scott Marshall asked me to collect something for him.'

The woman folded a towel and stared back at Venus.

'What is it?' she asked. 'I can get it for you.'

Venus shook her head quickly. 'It's something on his computer. It'll be quite hard to access, so it's best if I do it. He told me his room number – 424.'

The woman frowned.

'I know it's a pain, but it would help me SO much,'

pleaded Venus. 'It's my first film job.'

The woman sighed. 'All right,' she muttered, 'you can go in, but be quick.'

'Thanks,' said Venus, beaming gratefully.

The woman ambled down the corridor with her and inserted a card into the key slot of room 424. There was a click and then a green light flashed. The woman turned the handle and pushed it open. 'There you go,' she said, 'but remember – in and out.'

Venus nodded solemnly as the woman headed back to her trolley.

Venus let the heavy door close behind her and faced Scott Marshall's suite. This clearly wasn't your average hotel room; this was a vast apartment with several doors and passages leading off from the central area.

She ran over and checked the first door. It led to a plush bathroom. The second opened on to a bedroom.

With the third door she struck gold.

It led to a large, airy drawing room with an enormous window on the far wall. But the most important thing to Venus was the computer that was situated on a very large and grand mahogany desk. Venus was delighted to see that the machine was logged on.

Flicking on the desk lamp, she sat down in front of the computer. She quickly scanned all of the folders on the desktop and then did a file search with the words *AS2*

Budget. This produced nothing so she typed *AS2 Costs*. Again nothing. *AS2 Money*, *AS2 Spending*, and *AS2 Accounts* all drew blanks.

Venus was starting to feel a bit desperate and she racked her brains for the next search. *AS2 Finances*, she typed. After a thirty-second search, a whole list of files appeared on the screen.

Venus clicked on the first file.

It was entitled *Quarry Lighting Costs*, and was a spreadsheet. There were over a hundred pieces of kit itemised with prices beside them. This was just the sort of thing she was after, somewhere Marshall could have altered the costs. Venus whipped out a memory stick from her jacket pocket and plugged it into a USB port at the back of the computer. Immediately, she started copying the finance files on to the memory stick, working methodically down the list. She had nearly completed the last file, when she suddenly heard a noise from outside the room. She peered out of the door and was just in time to see a silhouetted figure lowering themselves down from an open window. It was the window above the narrow ledge, leading to the window in the corridor. Whoever it was must be seriously agile or have zero concern for their safety. She pelted back into the room, praying they hadn't spotted her. She was certain from their shape and build that the figure wasn't Scott

Marshall. Besides, why on earth would he want to break into his own hotel room?

Instantly, Venus grabbed the memory stick and flicked off the desk light.

Feeling panic setting in, Venus desperately scanned the room. She held her breath as she squashed herself up as tightly as she could into the only possible hiding place – under the desk. Footsteps then sounded in the room and the desk light was flicked on. All Venus could see of the person was their black trainers and the bottom of their jeans. If they looked down, they'd spot her instantly.

She then heard the clicking of computer keys and quiet, steady breathing. Time seemed to stop as Venus clenched her fists tightly and prayed she wouldn't be discovered.

And then, suddenly, the desk light was extinguished and Venus saw the feet hurrying back out of the door. She peered out and caught a very brief glimpse of the person's back – they were wearing a green sweatshirt and a blue baseball cap. She waited ten seconds before quickly jumping out from under the desk and turning the desk light on again.

Venus was torn. Should she pursue whoever it was that had just been in here or check out what it was they'd been looking at?

She went for the latter.

She clicked on *Recent Documents*.

Scott Marshall's diary appeared.

Venus shook her head uncertainly. Who would want to look at Marshall's diary?

She studied the screen. All of Marshall's day-to-day filming commitments were in black, but there were three items in blue – apparently corresponding to arrangements not directly connected to his filming schedule:

Friday: 5.20 p.m. – Dentist
Saturday: 6.30 p.m. – Le Cadre
Sunday: 11.45 a.m. – M. Nixon, suit fitting

Venus closed the program, flicked off the light and ran out of the door.

Do I still have a chance of catching up with the intruder?

She hurried out through the main part of the suite, into the empty corridor. One of the lifts was indicated as just reaching the third floor, going down, so she hit the stairs. Crashing down at top speed, she emerged at the bottom into the hotel lobby just as the baseball cap intruder was heading out through the revolving doors.

Venus started to run towards the doors, but a bellboy wheeling an enormous luggage trolley blocked her way.

'Let me through!' she snarled, but he had already stopped it, so Venus had to run round him, losing a few seconds.

Passing through the revolving doors, to her horror, she saw that the person's baseball cap had been replaced with a crash helmet and that they were clambering on to a red motorbike and gunning the engine.

They're going to get away and I'll lose my only lead.

At that second Venus spotted another motorbike, this one silver. Its engine was gently purring and its owner was standing beside it, checking the contents of their rucksack and talking to someone on their mobile.

Venus made a snap decision.

Leaping forward, she stooped down, grabbed a helmet from the pavement and pulled it on. Two seconds later, she was on the silver bike.

The guy who owned it realised what was happening too late. 'HEY!' he yelled as Venus revved the engine and pulled away from the kerb. 'HEY! What on earth do you think you are doing? STOP!'

Venus didn't look back. Dennis had taught her how to ride a motorbike on the set of *Monsoon Speed*; she just hoped she could remember everything. She pulled out on to the main road and saw the red bike about seventy metres ahead of her at some traffic lights. As they turned green, the bike accelerated sharply.

Venus gritted her teeth and sped forward at full throttle. She was gaining on the red bike, going as fast as she reckoned she could. Whatever she did, she mustn't lose them. Whoever was on that bike could be vital to the investigation.

At a crossroads, the red bike turned left. Venus followed it round seconds later. They were now on a residential road, terraced houses rushing past them. The red bike turned right on to a busy road. It weaved in and out of traffic and Venus followed suit, totally determined not to let it out of her sight.

Venus heard a heavy juggernaut behind her and felt the strong wind as it overtook her, nearly throwing her on to the pavement at the side of the road. But she stayed upright and pressed on, feeling the sweat covering her body as she began to catch up with the red bike. She closed the gap to twenty metres, then to fifteen. She'd be on to them in a few seconds. What would she do then? Leap across and knock them off? Don't be ridiculous. Overtake them and try to block their path? A possibility. However she did it, she had to stop them and confront them – nothing else would do.

Up ahead, the red bike entered a narrow alleyway and Venus pursued it. But moments later, two things happened. Firstly, the driver of the red bike turned round for the first time and spotted Venus.

Secondly, the wailing of a siren abruptly cut through the air, giving Venus a strong jolt of shock. She checked her side mirror and saw a police van speeding straight after her. It was about a hundred metres behind, but was gaining rapidly.

Disaster!

The owner of the silver bike had obviously called the police immediately and they were on her case.

She thought frantically for a few seconds about what to do. Carry on following the red bike and get the hackles of the police up while trying to evade arrest for nicking the bike? Or pull in and face the music?

She looked round at the police van. It would reach her in seconds. With a massive twist of regret, Venus applied the brakes and pulled the silver bike over. Sure enough, almost immediately, the police van screeched to a halt right next to her.

Venus swallowed nervously, switched off the engine and climbed off the bike. She opened her mouth to begin her speech begging for leniency, but to her surprise, four officers jumped out of the van and ran straight up a walkway leading to a low-rise block of flats.

Venus's mouth hung open.

They hadn't been after her at all. They were on a completely different call. She spun round and looked at the road up ahead where the red bike had gone. About fifty metres further on there was a mini-roundabout with three possible exits. The bike was nowhere to be seen.

Venus cursed herself.

I can't believe I just let it go. My one lead and I blew it!

Muttering furiously to herself, she pulled out her mobile and speed-dialled a number.

'Dennis,' she began, 'I think I might need a little bit of help.'

FRIDAY

Venus's mobile rang at six a.m.

'I can't believe you stole that bike,' Dennis began angrily.

'I thought we went over this yesterday,' Venus replied croakily, sitting up in bed and groaning when she saw the time on her bedside clock. 'I didn't *steal* it, I *borrowed* it.'

Dennis had responded quickly to her emergency call the day before and, thanks to his friend DCI Carla Radcliff, they'd traced the owner of the bike. Two of Radcliff's officers had returned it, claiming it had been used for police business.

'It was irresponsible and dangerous,' fumed Dennis. 'You could have got yourself killed.'

'Well I didn't, did I?' shot back Venus. 'And I was only doing it to try to find out what's going on with Scott Marshall. I'm just trying to help Elliot!'

Dennis sighed. 'Look, I know the last few weeks have been very hard, with your dad reappearing and everything, but you're still only fourteen and sometimes I've got to steer you in the right direction. I don't want you doing anything like that again. We're lucky Radcliff stepped in and smoothed things over.'

What is it about my grandfather and DCI Radcliff? He thinks she's the greatest person on earth.

'Yes, Granddad,' sighed Venus. 'Does DCI Radcliff have any idea who was on the red bike and why they were snooping around Marshall's hotel room?'

'No, she needed more to go on than you had; a partial numberplate wasn't enough,' answered Dennis. Venus cursed herself. She'd been too busy focusing on the bike to take in all its details.

'Well, can I go back to sleep then, please?'

'Yes,' he replied, 'but not for long. Elliot has spent the whole night going over the files you downloaded from Scott Marshall's computer. He's cross-referenced them with loads of other stuff and wants you round here at eight-thirty.'

Venus rubbed her eyes wearily. 'OK, I'll be there.'

As soon as Venus entered Dennis's apartment, Elliot called out to her. 'You've done great work, Venus; I think together we've cracked it.'

Elliot was sitting in front of a laptop on Dennis's kitchen table, surrounded by piles of papers. Dennis was sitting next to him. Venus hurried over and looked down to the table. Elliot was scrolling through pages and pages of accounts.

'You've nailed Marshall?' she asked, sitting down.

'I'll explain,' said Elliot.

At last, a result! All of my investigative work has paid off!

'For ages, the files you downloaded just looked like normal spreadsheets of costs,' began Elliot. 'I thought we were on a wild goose chase, but — '

'The Cribben-Taylors were right?' butted in Venus. 'You've got them their proof?'

'No, it's not like that.'

Venus was stunned. 'Well, what *is* it like?' she demanded.

Elliot took a deep breath. 'At about five this morning, I was on the verge of giving up, but then I found this tiny paragraph hidden away in one of the earlier documents.'

'What did it say?'

'In these initial calculations, Marshall made a simple error. He mistook pounds for dollars.'

'What do you mean?'

'He wrote down a whole list of figures in dollar amounts not pound amounts – but said they were pound figures. If one pound roughly equals two dollars, then when you write down figures in dollars but you mistakenly call them pounds, it looks like you're spending twice as much as you really are. When he wrote that something cost two thousand pounds, it actually cost two thousand *dollars* – which is nearer to *one* thousand pounds.'

'Oh my God,' said Venus, 'you mean this whole thing is just . . . just . . . a clerical error?'

'Exactly!' cut in Dennis. 'Marshall's spending looks outrageously high – that's why the Cribben-Taylors became suspicious. But he's actually spent half of that amount!'

'But Marshall is a totally experienced film guy,' Venus pointed out. 'How could he make such a stupid mistake?'

Elliot sighed. 'It's called working under intense pressure. Once he wrote down those initial figures, he's been making the same mistake ever since. Either he has no idea what he's done or he's so embarrassed by his earlier error that he's just carrying on and hoping they don't notice.'

'But what about the phonecall I heard him make when I was on the horse-riding shoot – you know . . . the one about getting the money or going to jail?' asked Venus.

'I have no idea,' replied Elliot, 'but I'm pretty certain now that it has nothing to do with ripping off the *AS2* budget.'

'Well, what about the hotel-room intruder?'

'It's certainly suspicious, but it doesn't look like it's

connected to our investigation,' replied Elliot.

Venus's head was swirling with confusion. If Marshall wasn't involved in a financial scam, then who had whacked her on the back of her head in his Winnebago? And who had sent her the *Back Off* note? And possibly interfered with the water computer? None of it made any sense to her.

Then something else suddenly struck Venus. 'Hang on a sec,' she murmured. 'If Marshall is in the clear, does that mean you're going back to the States now, Elliot?'

Elliot sucked in a deep breath. 'It does, Venus. I'm sorry, but I have another job to do back home and I have to get cracking on it.'

I can't believe it. He comes over to England, steps into the centre of my life and then goes off again. Talk about messing around with someone's head.

'Is that it then? Are you going to disappear from my life again?'

'Absolutely not!' Elliot insisted. 'I'll keep in touch weekly – daily, if you like.'

'But what about Mum?' demanded Venus. 'What if she finds out I'm in contact with you behind her back? She's bound to wise up sooner or later.'

'That's a very hard one,' admitted Elliot, 'but to be honest, I don't think you or I are ready for her to know. I think we should get to know each other a bit better before we tell her, because telling her will be very, very difficult.'

Venus thought about this and nodded. She couldn't bear it if her mum found out about her and Elliot and forbade Venus from ever seeing or speaking to him again. What if Gail presented Venus with an ultimatum: your father or me? She shivered at the thought.

Venus took a sip from her bottle of water and put it down on a table. She looked up at the long, rickety, rope bridge, stretched between two fake rocks, with a painted pool of lava below. This was to be her last scene in *AS2*. She, Indigo and Brad had to run across the bridge, pursued by a deadly mercenary whose sole task was to kill them.

'OK, guys,' called Ed Fry, 'we're ready. Venus, Indigo, Brad – places at the start of the bridge. Jordan – into position.'

The three teenagers walked over to the piece of jutting-out rock at the far end of the bridge. Jordan, the stunt guy doubling for the mercenary, winked at them and strode over to his starting point.

'That guy gives me the creeps,' whispered Indigo. 'He's more muscle man than human. I bet he takes a hundred daily food supplements.'

Venus and Brad laughed. Indigo was spot on.

There was five minutes of discussion between Fry and some tech people and then everything was ready.

'And – ACTION!'

Venus knew every centimetre of the bridge. Ed Fry had gone across it with them plank by plank. So she knew exactly where to put her feet and how to get to the other side without toppling over. Jordan was to have no such luxury. He would chase them nearly to the end and then plunge off the bridge and into the 'burning pool' below.

Venus's feet crashed over the ground and on to the swaying bridge, with Indigo and Brad less than a metre behind her. Venus sped forward, concentrating a hundred per cent on placing her feet exactly, hitting each plank with a dull echoing sound.

Jordan was catching them up as planned and when they reached the halfway point, he lunged at Indigo's feet but missed her. Venus sprinted on, focusing solely on the bridge's end.

As they reached the three-quarter point, Jordan flew forward towards Indigo.

Indigo stepped sharply out of the way and Venus kicked out, catching him on the shoulder. With a great cry, he staggered for a few metres and then dramatically tumbled over the side on to an unseen crash mat.

Venus, Indigo and Brad sprinted on and made it to the other side, still running until they heard Fry's voice.

'CUT!' he shouted.

They drifted back towards where Fry was standing and

joined him in checking the footage on his monitor.

'Looking great!' he said, smiling when he was satisfied that the take was good enough.

Venus breathed an immense sigh of relief. Her last stunt on *AS2* and she'd got it in one take!

'I guess that's it for you guys,' said Fry, grinning. 'Well done! You've all worked really hard. May our paths cross again!'

He shook their hands and asked Indigo to hang back for a second for a quick word. Venus and Brad walked slowly over to the trestle table under which they'd left their bags. Venus slung her red and black record bag over her shoulder and reached for Indigo's green and blue rucksack. She picked it up and was surprised at how heavy it was.

'What the hell do you think you're doing?'

Venus turned round.

Indigo had caught up with them and was staring at Venus furiously.

'Er . . . I was just going to give your bag to you,' replied Venus, taken aback at Indigo's sudden bout of rage.

Indigo reached out and clutched the bag to her chest. Her expression immediately softened. 'Sorry, Venus. I didn't mean to bite your head off . . . I just hate it when people touch my things.'

Venus pulled a half-smile. 'Yeah . . . cool . . . whatever,' she replied, still shocked by Indigo's rant.

'Let's have one last coffee,' said Indigo with a smile, back to her usual friendly self.

'Definitely,' agreed Brad.

Ten minutes later, they were sitting by the catering van, sipping cappucinos.

'So what are you up to next, Indigo?' asked Brad.

Indigo sighed. 'I've got exams next year; that's what I'm up to. We've already started doing the mock papers and it's driving me absolutely mad!'

'And you're taking a gap year after school, aren't you?' asked Venus.

'A gap year?' exclaimed Indigo. 'How about ten gap years? I'm going to do stunt jobs, save up money and go travelling, and then repeat that process hopefully for ever!'

'Sounds like a great plan. It's been an amazing week,' said Venus.

'Yeah,' Brad said, nodding. 'You did so well! I can't believe it was your first stunt job!'

Venus blushed.

'He's right,' said Indigo, 'you've done brilliantly.'

'Cheers, guys.'

They chatted for another twenty minutes and then all agreed it was time to go. They walked to the front entrance of the studios together and realised they were each taking a separate bus. After much hugging and laughter and swapping of phone numbers, they said their good-byes.

Venus's bus arrived first. She waved at them through the window until they were out of sight.

What an incredible experience! I can't believe I've got school next week. What a comedown!

Dennis and Elliot were clearing up Dennis's living room. Elliot was shredding documents while Dennis rearranged the furniture.

'I have one update,' announced Elliot as Venus walked in. 'I had someone looking into Scott Marshall's private life, his finances and stuff, and they'd delivered absolutely nothing. But I've just got an email from them saying that Marshall's wife owes a huge amount of money. The reason we didn't find out about this earlier is because she operates a very complicated set of bank accounts, many in the Cayman Islands, which are very hard to trace. My contact finally managed to follow a trail that links her to a loan. That must have been what Marshall was talking about on the phone when you saw him on Hampstead Heath.'

Venus nodded. 'That explains that phonecall,' she agreed, 'but we still don't know who the hotel intruder is. Shouldn't we tell the police?'

'I've already mentioned it to DCI Radcliff,' said Dennis,

'and she's going to have a look into it.'

Enough of Radcliff! She seems to be everywhere in my granddad's life, but he won't tell me how they met or what they 'worked on' in the past. He's as bad as Elliot with these secrets!

'Anyway, good work, Venus,' said Elliot, smiling broadly. 'I can't believe what you've been through this week and yet here you are really positive, not ground down by any of it.'

'What's the point of being down about things? OK, I was threatened and nearly drowned, but there are far worse things that can happen.'

For a second there was absolute silence and then the three of them burst out laughing like a pack of cackling hyenas.

'You really are something, aren't you?' Elliot grinned, lightly squeezing her shoulder.

Venus could only blush.

SATURDAY

Venus stirred her cup of coffee. She and Kate were sitting at an outside table of a small café on the high street.

'So that's it?' asked Kate. 'Case closed?'

Venus brushed a stray strand of hair out of her face. 'I guess so,' she replied. 'At least we put Marshall in the clear. If we'd got the police involved there'd have been a serious amount of egg on the Cribben-Taylors' faces, not to mention Elliot's.'

'But the other stuff is still a mystery, right?'

'Yeah, looks that way.'

'So you'll never find out who sent you that note?'

Venus sighed. 'You don't think it could be . . . ?'

'What, Franco?' asked Kate.

Venus nodded.

'Why would Franco send you a note at Elstree Studios telling you to back off? You're not on his case. Yes, you're scared that he might show up again one day, but you certainly aren't going to go looking for him. And anyway, it probably wasn't him on that CCTV camera – their quality is terrible. I bet it was like the time at the castle when you were sure that guy was Franco and it wasn't. You're still a bit traumatised by it all – who wouldn't be? You were there when his mum died and you nearly killed him. That's enough to spook out anyone big time.'

They were quiet for a few seconds. A toddler sped past them on a scooter, with a harried mother chasing behind him.

'Let's forget about Franco and all of that stunt stuff for a minute and focus on what really matters,' said Kate. 'What are you going to wear tonight?'

In all of the madness, Venus had completely forgotten about the premiere of the first *Airborne Sword* movie. Dennis, as stunt co-ordinator on that film, had managed to pull some strings and got Elliot a ticket too. Venus was really pleased about this, but she'd hardly given any thought to the one crucial aspect – clothes.

'What do you reckon?' she asked Kate. 'The turquoise dress or the black mini-skirt and beaded halterneck top?'

Kate pondered this question. 'I think the turquoise dress,' she replied. 'You could wear it with that amazing opal necklace your mum got you for your last birthday.'

'Yeah,' agreed Venus. 'What about shoes?'

'Shoes are a bit harder,' said Kate thoughtfully. 'I'd better come to your's for a full fashion show.'

Venus smiled. 'That's *exactly* what I need.'

Venus and Kate spent a few of hours with an ever-increasing mound of clothes and shoes on the bed and all over the floor. Venus had gone off the turquoise dress, but it was now firmly back in favour and then had to try various shoes – finally settling on a pair of cream strappy heels.

When Kate left, Venus thanked her profusely for all of her fashion advice, and then hung her dress in a protective bag and put her shoes and jewellery in a box.

She grabbed some toast and was about to go to Dennis's, as arranged, when Gail walked in.

'Hey Mum, how did your meeting go?'

Gail had agreed to another work meeting on a Saturday afternoon. Venus had raised her concerns about Gail working too hard once again.

'It was OK,' Gail replied, 'but where are you going? I thought I'd cook us something special tonight.'

'Mum!' tutted Venus. 'It's the film premiere tonight. You know, the one Dennis is taking me to – *Airborne Sword?* I was watching the sequel being filmed this week.'

Gail nodded her head. 'Of course; sorry, my brain is all over the place. What time will you be back?'

'Twelve at the latest. Dennis will bring me home. Is that OK?'

'That's fine, but make sure it's no later or you and Dennis will both be for the chop.'

'Yes, Mum.'

'And I'll cook for us tomorrow night,' added Gail. 'We'll have a long girlie session. I want to know everything you've been up to this week.'

Venus gave her mum a smile. 'No worries, and you'll tell me all about your case?'

'Do you really want to hear about it?'

'Of course, Mum. You know I'm intrigued by it all.'

'Intrigued enough to follow me into the profession?' enquired Gail hopefully.

'Mum, give it a rest!' said Venus, laughing. 'I'm fourteen!'

Gail laughed too. 'Yes, you're right,' she replied, 'I promise I won't ask you again . . . at least not for a week!'

Venus gave her mum a quick hug and left the house.

It was four o'clock when Venus rang on Dennis's front door. The premiere wasn't till eight p.m.

Elliot opened it.

'Hey Elliot, how's it going? Where's Granddad?'

'Dennis isn't here,' Elliot replied. 'He had to meet someone. He's coming later and then we'll all go to the premiere together. I'm just in the middle of making some calls,' he said, heading for the bedroom.

'Cool,' answered Venus, ambling over to the computer and logging on to check her email and kill time before Dennis arrived.

Venus spent some time checking and responding to emails, then began browsing the Internet. She checked Kelly Tanner's homepage and a couple of good stunt sites. She looked at various links to the *Airborne Sword* premiere, and then Scott Marshall's homepage. As she was scrolling down his films, she came across a mention of *Beast Survival* – she remembered it as being the film in which the serious stunt accident had happened. Dennis had never finished telling her about it. There were thousands of hits when she Googled it and she browsed through them until she came to some stuff about the accident. There was a picture of the wrecked set focusing on a vast, twisted length of metal.

'That must be the lighting rig that exploded,' murmured Venus to herself.

There was a newspaper article about the tragedy. Venus scanned the article:

Two technicians and one stuntman were killed . . . David Forrest died when the lighting rig exploded . . . Forrest's family tried to sue producer Scott Marshall . . . blamed him for the deaths . . . judge threw out the case before it came to court . . .

Forrest's family blamed Scott Marshall for Dave's death? That was interesting. She Googled *David Forrest*. There were a couple of profiles and a memorial site for him. Venus opened up a mini-biography and studied the films he'd been in before the tragedy. When she clicked on the family page she found several photographs of Dave

Forrest at home and on holiday – the usual family album stuff. He had long blond hair and a moustache. The site included a moving tribute from his daughter, Suzie, but it ended on a bitter note:

Dad meant everything to us. We all thought the world of him. After he died, it all fell apart. Mum became totally depressed and my little brother got into drugs. It completely destroyed us.

Venus sighed heavily. She knew what it was like to grow up without a dad, but luckily she'd got hers back. Suzie Forrest didn't have that opportunity.

When Venus scrolled down there were more tributes and painful statements from family members. There was a consistent theme: the Forrest family held Scott Marshall responsible for Dave Forrest's death, whatever the judge had ruled.

Venus took another look at the photos. There was one of Dave with a girl of about seven on his shoulders. The caption read, *Dad and Suzie.*

'Poor girl,' muttered Venus to herself. Suzie would be – what? – seventeen now.

Something about the photograph caught her eye and she zoomed in on the photograph of Suzie.

'Oh my God,' Venus said with a start.

It was in the eyes and the nose and the shape of Suzie's chin. They were just the same as Indigo's . . .

Indigo!

Venus's first reaction was one of total confusion. Poor, poor Indigo. She'd mentioned that her dad had died, but their conversation had been interrupted. Why had she felt she had to change her name? Well, she'd obviously forgiven Marshall now as she was happy to work on one of his films . . .

At that second, a deep sense of unease overcame Venus.

When she first checked out Scott Marshall's Winnebago, who had startled her? Indigo.

Who was so surprised to see her at the gig, and kept staring at her head? Indigo.

Venus felt her hands going clammy as a deep twist of anxiety turned in her chest.

Another memory crashed into Venus's brain. Indigo's rucksack. When Venus had picked it up, Indigo had reacted savagely – it was a really extreme reaction. It was only a rucksack after all . . . wasn't it?

And then suddenly Venus remembered the intruder in Scott Marshall's room. This person had managed to get in using that very narrow ledge. Only a very experienced climber or stunt artist would ever dream of attempting a break-in using that route. Who had those skills? Indigo. So it must have been Indigo who was telling Venus to back off in that note. Back off from what?

A vision of Marshall's computer screen returned to Venus: *Saturday 6.30 p.m. – Le Cadre.*

'Oh my God!' exclaimed Venus, louder this time.

'What is it?' asked Elliot, wandering over.

'What's *Le Cadre*, Elliot?'

'It's that French restaurant by the Thames. Why?'

'Scott Marshall's going to *Le Cadre* at six-thirty,' she replied.

'That wouldn't be surprising,' replied Elliot. 'Marshall always takes his whole family out for a meal before the premiere of one of his films. It's a tradition.'

The colour completely drained from Venus's face. She took a deep breath and she filled him in on everything she'd just found out.

'So you think Indigo – Suzie – is plotting some sort of confrontation at *Le Cadre*?' Elliot said, once she'd finished.

'Well, it's certainly a possibility,' Venus replied. 'Should we call the police?'

Elliot shook his head. 'If the police turn up and she's there, she might panic and do something stupid.'

'So we go there?' asked Venus, reaching for her jacket.

Elliot grabbed his keys and hurried to the door. 'It's our only option,' he replied. 'It's six o'clock – we have half an hour.'

Fifteen seconds later they were down in the street desperately trying to flag down a cab. The first two already had passengers.

'Come on, come on!' urged Venus.

The third cab pulled over for them.

'*Le Cadre* restaurant,' said Elliot. 'There's an extra twenty pounds in it for you if you can get us there in record time.'

The ride was tense and silent. What would they find when they got there?

The cabbie clearly knew London well because nineteen minutes later he deposited them at the end of a small road connected to a cobbled walkway that spread alongside a brick wall overlooking the River Thames.

'It's just round the corner,' the cabbie informed them.

Elliot handed him the fare and the speed bonus as he and Venus leaped out of the cab. They ran round the corner and found themselves on the walkway. The river was to their left. On their right was a row of upmarket cafés and restaurants.

They sprinted past *Café Unique*, *The Bull and Pit* and *Risorgimento*. The fourth building was *Le Cadre*. There was a doorman stationed by its front door. He was wearing dark glasses and a jet-black suit. Unsurprisingly, he was built like a bouncer.

Venus and Elliot hurried over to the door.

The doorman instinctively blocked their path, a protective guardian of an exclusive establishment.

'We have to get in there,' said Venus, peering anxiously over the guy's shoulder.

'Sorry,' he replied, 'this is a private club and only members can enter.'

'This is an emergency,' Elliot explained.

The doorman gave him a funny look. 'What kind of emergency?' he demanded.

'It's too complicated to go into right now,' said Venus testily. Please just let us in.'

'Listen,' said Elliot, with desperation creeping into his voice, 'you've got to let us in. If you don't, something terrible might happen.'

The man's eyes flickered for a second, but the resolute expression stayed on his face. 'If you're not from the emergency services and you have nothing to show or tell me outlining this "emergency", then you can't come in.'

Elliot clenched his fist and took a step forward, but Venus grabbed him by the arm and dragged him away. The doorman's eyes followed them suspiciously.

'He'll never budge,' hissed Venus. 'We'll have to get in another way.'

'You're right,' agreed Elliot, 'let's cut round the back.'

They hurried off over the cobbles. As they turned the corner Venus stole a backward glance. The doorman had turned his gaze away from them and was looking out over the Thames. Venus and Elliot dipped into the narrow service road at the rear of the cafés and restaurants. They ran along it until they came to the back of *Le Cadre*.

'How's your climbing?' asked Elliot, looking up at the smooth façade of the building.

'OK,' replied Venus, grabbing on to the bottom of a drainpipe and shinning up it. Elliot was right behind her. Seconds later, they found themselves looking through a barred window on the first floor. Inside was a series of round tables with wealthy-looking diners.

'That's not them,' hissed Elliot.

They skirted past the window and, using drainpipes and jutting-out bricks for support, made it to the second floor.

'No,' said Venus, looking through a window at two staid, middle-aged couples.

Up they went again.

They pulled themselves up on a sill.

Third floor.

As Venus peered through the window she could see what looked like the back of Scott Marshall's greying head. There were two teenage boys and a girl, a rather glamorous woman, an elderly couple – his parents perhaps – and there was much noise of chatting and laughter emanating from the room.

'Let's just get up on the roof and see if we can get in that way,' Elliot hissed from behind her.

Venus soon pulled herself up on to the long flat roof. At the far left were two green doors about ten metres apart, and some big dustbins opposite them.

There, heading towards a doorway, was Indigo.

'Oh my God!' Indigo exclaimed in horror. 'What the hell are you doing here, Venus?'

Venus swallowed anxiously. 'We know about your dad,' said Venus, glancing sideways at Elliot who was slowly pulling himself up. 'We know about the explosion on *Beast Survival* . . . We know it all . . . Suzie.'

Indigo bristled at the use of her real name. 'Stay away from me!' she yelled, edging sideways to the line of four giant metal dustbins. This Indigo, with her hard, inpenetrable expression, seemed to bear no resemblance to the Indigo who Venus had come to regard as a friend.

'We know why you're here,' said Venus.

'You know nothing!' Indigo shouted. 'I'm the one who knows what's happening. You just got in the way. What were you doing in Marshall's Winnebago? You were snooping around and I kept trying to warn you off. You just wouldn't take the hint.'

Venus suddenly remembered the water tank incident. 'Was messing with the computer system and nearly killing me a hint?' she snapped.

'I didn't want to *kill* you!' yelled Indigo. 'I tried to warn you with the horse.'

'You knew Prince was a difficult horse to handle?' whispered Venus.

Indigo nodded. 'You said you were a weak rider when

we were chatting. I honked the car horn and hoped Prince would bolt. I thought you'd fall off and break your arm or something. I didn't plan on you being able to continue with the shoot – and carry on prying. None of this has anything to do with you; it's between me and Scott Marshall. So back off and take whoever he is with you.' She pointed towards Elliot, who was getting to his knees.

Venus shook her head. 'We want to help you.'

Indigo laughed sarcastically. 'Help me?'

'We know that your family think the explosion could have been avoided. We know you think it was Scott Marshall's fault.'

'It *was* his fault!' snarled Indigo. 'And he got away with it. That stupid judge kicked the case out before it even started. He should have spent the last ten years behind bars.'

Venus took a small step forward. 'I can totally understand how you feel,' she said softly.

'No you can't!' snapped Indigo with a furious glare, stepping closer to the bins. 'I was only seven at the time. Can you imagine what my dad's death did to me and my family? We had a good life before he was killed. We were happy. That man RUINED our lives. And he's just sitting down there with his happy family.' She looked furious.

'So you're going to get your own back on him?' asked Venus, trying to keep her talking as Elliot moved slowly sideways to Indigo.

'And the rest!' snarled Indigo. 'I've paid for his criminal irresponsibility for the last ten years. It's now time for him to pay.'

'Come on, Indigo,' urged Venus, 'I'm sure the three of us can work out something that suits everyone.'

'It's too late for that!' shouted Indigo.

'Why?' asked Venus, edging a step closer. 'What are you going to do?'

At that second, Venus saw Indigo glancing nervously at the bins.

'Listen,' said Venus, her voice beginning to quiver slightly. 'We don't have to go to the police. We can do this ourselves.'

At that second, Elliot sprang forward and made a lunge for Indigo. But Indigo reacted instantly, aiming a vicious kick at his stomach. Her boot made a crunching impact. He stumbled a few steps, his body wobbling. As he backpedalled, the heel of his left foot hit a raised piece of stone.

Venus lurched forward to grab him. But it was too late.

Elliot's body tumbled backwards and he toppled over the side of the roof.

'NOOOOOOOOOOO!' screamed Venus. No one could survive a fall from that height.

She saw the look of shock and terror on Indigo's face. In spite of the agony Venus felt at that second, she took advantage of Indigo's lowered guard and leaped towards her, aiming a flying kick at her chest. Indigo toppled backwards but managed to get in a punch to Venus's face. Venus's cheek stung madly in pain but she leaped on top of Indigo and pinned her down. Indigo rolled sideways to gather momentum, then managed to fling Venus off her and along the rooftop.

Venus rolled over and held her arms over her face as Indigo's boot came smashing towards her. She flipped back to her feet and as Indigo kicked out again, Venus caught her right boot in her hand and twisted it sharply, turning Indigo's whole body over and to the ground in front of her. She fell badly and clutched her left ankle in agony.

As tears streamed down Venus's cheeks, she jumped over Indigo's horizontal body and reached for the nearest of the metal dustbins. She pulled the bin to one side. Nothing.

'NO, VENUS!' Indigo screamed, 'JUST GET AWAY – WHILE YOU CAN!'

She yanked the second bin, quickly checking that Indigo was still down. She was lying there, clutching her ankle and writhing in pain. There was nothing to see behind that bin either.

But tucked behind the third bin was Indigo's blue and green rucksack, the one she'd freaked out over when Venus had picked it up.

Venus grabbed it and carefully undid the zip.

'NO, VENUS!' screamed Indigo.

At that second, Venus felt the whole world caving in on her. Inside Indigo's rucksack was a small black box with a series of multicoloured wires protruding from it and a digital timer on the front.

'Oh my God,' whispered Venus as she studied the timer. It blinked back. *41, 40.*

It's a BOMB!

Of course! Dave Forrest died in an explosion and now Indigo wanted Scott Marshall to meet the same fate.

38, 37.

She'd seen Indigo walking around with the rucksack, so it must be safe to move it. Venus grabbed the box and kicked open the door, leading to the restaurant.

Venus pelted down the stairs, holding the box out in front of her as if its very touch was poisoning her fingers.

22.

Come on! Come on!

She reached the ground floor and sped towards the front door.

If I don't make it, everyone in here – including me – could die!

The officious doorman turned round on hearing her footsteps.

17, 16.

'How the hell — ' started the doorman.

'*Get out of the way!*' Venus barged him aside and leaped through the doorway.

13.

She knew exactly where she was going.

11, 10.

Faster! Go faster!

Venus reached the stone wall.

8, 7.

Using every remaining ounce of strength in her body, she threw the box over the wall.

5, 4.

It arced through the air. The second it smacked into the river, it exploded. A gigantic wave of Thames water crashed upwards, its spray completely drenching Venus.

Venus watched as plumes of purple smoke curled up from the black box and it began to sink. A few seconds later, it had disappeared beneath the surface.

Relief washed over Venus, but then she suddenly remembered Elliot and a surge of pain swelled inside her chest.

Shaking violently, Venus somehow managed to pull her mobile out of her jacket pocket. With trembling fingers she speed-dialled a number from the phone's memory. It rang a couple of times before a female voice answered. 'DCI Carla Radcliff speaking.'

'It's Venus Spring. I think you should come to a restaurant called *Le Cadre*, by the Thames, immediately.'

'You sound terrible, Venus,' said Radcliff. 'What's going on?'

But Venus had already killed the call.

She slumped on to a wooden bench and held her face in her hands, the tears streaming down her face. Suzie Forrest – the girl who had been up on that roof because her father had been killed – had ended up killing Venus's father. It was a terrible, tragic twist of fate.

Venus's whole body shook with agony and despair. She'd only just got to know him and now he'd been ripped away from her. It was so unfair!

When a hand grabbed her shoulder, she gave a massive jolt and spun round, half expecting it to be Indigo.

But it wasn't Indigo.

It was Elliot.

Venus stared up at him in electrifying shock. He slid down on to the bench next to her and held her tightly. Venus nestled against his chest and sobbed uncontroll-ably. One solitary word managed to squeeze out of her mouth.

'*Dad.*'

Eventually, Elliot released her from his grasp.

'I landed on a skip,' he explained. 'Thank God the rubbish hadn't been collected! I'm badly bruised, but I think that's it.'

Venus wiped her eyes and looked at him, relief coursing through her entire body.

'You did an amazing job up there, Venus.' He smiled proudly. 'Utterly amazing. You just saved everyone in that building. I'm stunned. I've phoned Dennis and told him everything. He's called Carla Radcliff, who told him you'd already called. She's going to sort everything out.'

They were both suddenly alerted by a voice behind them.

It was the doorman from *Le Cadre*.

'Excuse me,' he began, 'but was that a . . . I mean . . . was it . . . you know . . .'

Elliot smiled and shook his head. 'It was only an exercise,' he replied jovially. 'This is my daughter. She's preparing for a very advanced cadet's course and one of the tasks was to get inside a building without using the front door. Sorry for any inconvenience.'

'But that black box in her hand,' whispered the guy, 'it looked like . . . like a bomb!'

Elliot looked at the man sympathetically. 'I told you, it was just an exercise, bit of play-acting . . . nothing more.'

'Oh,' said the doorman. He sounded disappointed.

'Another of our trainees is up on the roof at present,' explained Elliot. 'Some police officers will arrive to pick her up, but once again this is all part of the training process and there's absolutely nothing to worry about.'

The doorman shook his head in bewilderment.

'Well . . . OK then,' he replied slowly, 'thank you for telling me.'

'No problem,' said Elliot, smiling at him. 'Thank *you* for being understanding.'

The doorman nodded at them and hurried back over to his post, muttering to himself.

A few minutes later, Venus saw a sleek, black Mercedes sweep round the corner and pull up opposite *Le Cadre*. DCI Carla Radcliff and two plain-clothed officers climbed out.

Radcliff looked ice-cool and neat, as always, with a charcoal-grey trouser suit and her hair scraped back tightly from her face. She spoke to the doorman briefly and sent her two officers inside. She walked over to Venus and Elliot.

Elliot stood, walked towards her and gave her a massive hug.

Venus looked at them in shock.

First it's Dennis who's her best friend and now it's Elliot. This Radcliff connection gets weirder by the second. When are they going to tell me what's going on?

Radcliff stood back. 'Hello, Venus,' she said. 'I hear that once again you've been in the thick of the action and triumphed.'

Venus blushed. She associated Radcliff with trouble, but was pleased with the praise. Elliot sat back down next to

Venus. Radcliff leaned against the wall by the Thames and faced them.

'I wish you'd told me about this whole thing earlier,' she said. 'I'm surprised at you, Elliot.'

Elliot smiled and studied her face. 'It was a delicate job,' he replied. 'It needed a light touch.'

'Are you saying I'd have gone in heavy-handed?' demanded Radcliff, with a frown.

'It has been known,' replied Elliot.

Radcliff sighed and looked at father and daughter.

'Are you two OK?' she asked.

'We're fine,' Venus nodded. 'What are you going to do with Indigo – I mean, Suzie Forrest?'

At that second, the two police officers appeared with a hobbling Indigo wedged between them.

'I understand she's the girl whose father famously died in that stunt accident years ago. We'll take this into account, but to be honest, she's not in for an easy ride. If that bomb had gone off at the restaurant, it might not just have taken the Marshall family with it; it could have killed everyone in the building. So I think we could be looking at a very long sentence.'

Venus nodded. However much sympathy she had for Indigo and her pain over the death of her father, nothing justified blowing all those people up.

'How long are you in the UK?' Radcliff asked Elliot.

'I'm leaving tomorrow night,' he said, 'but I'll be back soon. Now I've made contact with Venus, I'll be turning up here quite a bit.'

'Good,' said Radcliff. 'Next time you come, look me up and we'll have a drink.'

'Sounds good,' said Elliot with a nod.

'Right then,' said Radcliff briskly, 'I'll get my officers to take statements from you both. We're going to keep this thing out of the public eye. People get slightly jittery when they hear of teenagers running around on restaurant rooftops with bombs in their hands.'

Their statements were taken beside the Mercedes. Venus looked in and saw a handcuffed, pale-faced Indigo sitting in the back. When they were all finished, the DCI shook Venus's and Elliot's hands.

'Don't forget to call me when you're next here,' she instructed Elliot.

Venus waited until Radcliff's car had disappeared from view and then spoke to her father. 'What is it with you, Granddad and DCI Radcliff? How do you both know her so well?'

Elliot eyed Venus warily. 'I worked with her when I was originally in London. Dennis got to know her through me. I thought there could have been a romantic liaison between them, but he says it never happened. No one ever could replace your grandma in Dennis's eyes.'

'What did you work on with her?' asked Venus.

'I'll tell you, but not now. I believe we have a premiere to attend.'

How many times can he avoid spilling the beans?

Venus checked her watch.

7.17. The premiere starts in less than an hour!

'We're never going to make it!' said Venus in horror. 'We have to get back to the flat and get changed and everything.'

'No we don't,' said Elliot, as the reassuring sound of Dennis's campervan engine purred and it appeared round the corner.

'Granddad!' shouted Venus, running to greet him. Dennis jumped out of the driver's seat and crushed her in a massive bear hug.

When he finally released her, he was shaking his head. 'How do you always get yourself into these impossibly dangerous scrapes, Venus?'

'Maybe I take after one or both of you two,' she said, grinning at him and Elliot.

Venus was first in the van. She emerged wearing the turquoise dress and strappy heels in no time. Elliot and Dennis took their turns and both stepped out looking rather dashing in their evening suits and bow ties.

'OK,' announced Dennis, 'let's make a move.'

Dennis drove a couple of miles and parked the van.

They then caught a taxi to Leicester Square, arriving outside the cinema at quarter to eight.

The square was crammed with people. Nervous excitement buzzed in the air. Outside the Empire cinema were thousands of fans making every effort to get as near as possible to the fencing. Security guards stood every ten metres, in their tuxedoes and tiny earpieces, making sure they stayed back.

Exhilaration bubbled away deliciously inside Venus; she had come before to gaze at the stars of a couple of movies along with the rest of the public, but tonight she wasn't going to be hanging around outside; tonight she was going in!

In the distance she could see the plush, red carpet leading up to the front of the cinema. A couple of black limousines had just arrived and their drivers were helping an array of stars out and on to the path towards the cinema entrance.

Dennis reached inside his jacket and pulled out three silver tickets. 'Come on,' he said, grinning.

The three of them walked towards a knot of security people and Dennis flashed the invitations. A security guy pulled a rope aside and his colleagues moved out of the way to let this new group in.

Venus couldn't believe it. There she was – through security and on her way! As she walked forward, she was almost blinded by the incessant flashing bulbs of cameras. The press were noisy as it was, but suddenly there was a crescendo of shouts.

'OVER HERE, SAFFRON!'

'HEY, SAFFRON!'

'GIVE US A POUT, SAFFRON!

Twenty metres ahead of Venus stood Saffron Ritchie – Hollywood legend and star of *Airbourne Sword*. The media pack was going completely berserk and Saffron was indulging them for a minute. The massed ranks of the press were a human forest of competing lenses.

Saffron gave the paparazzi one more dazzling smile and then headed into the building on the arm of her latest beau, Harvey Maynard – an actor ten years her junior and tipped for great things on the indie movie scene.

As Venus, Elliot and Dennis came parallel with the media scrum, a couple of flashbulbs popped.

Dennis laughed. 'They haven't got a clue who we are, but they're terrified they might miss us in case we're actually famous.'

Venus laughed and gave her most theatrical smile to the cameras.

'I thought you had no interest in stardom and being seen in the right places with the right people,' joked Dennis. 'I thought you always wanted to be the anonymous stunt artist!'

'I do,' replied Venus, 'but as the cameras are there, it would be rude not to smile!'

Dennis laughed and steered her towards the cinema's huge front entrance.

As they stepped inside, Venus opened her mouth with amazement. The entire place had been decked out like a huge airport hangar. There were giant models of planes at the sides of the room, the walls were adorned with maps and charts. People wearing flight uniforms were handing out drinks and canapés. The organisers had taken the airborne theme very, very seriously.

'Unreal,' gasped Venus.

Elliot and Dennis accepted glasses of champagne from one of the stewards. Venus was about to take one too, but Elliot shook his head. 'No chance, young lady, it's orange juice for you.'

'I was only going to try it.'

'You'll have plenty of chances to try it when you're older,' Dennis said firmly, handing her a glass of juice.

The foyer was awash with glitzy dresses, shining black suits and ties. The place smelled of perfume and aftershave. Venus recognised several actors from the film.

'That's Paulo Dante,' she said, pointing him out. Apparently he's a nightmare to work with.'

An announcement then rang out across the 'hangar'.

'Ladies and gentlemen,' said a deep, male voice. 'The

premiere of *Airborne Sword* will commence in five minutes. Would all guests please make their way to their allocated seats.'

Dennis checked their invites and led them to find their seats through an archway and into the enormous cavern that was the main cinema.

Venus had been looking forward to this night for ages. And even though she was still reeling from the day's events, she was determined to enjoy this experience.

Dennis gave her shoulder a squeeze.

'What do you reckon?' he smiled.

'Awesome,' replied Venus without hesitation.

Two minutes later, the main house lights went down and the sound of chattering and whispering stopped.

A single spotlight dipped on to the stage at the front and a familiar man, wearing an immaculate black suit and black bow tie, walked into its beam. Scott Marshall.

'He hasn't got a clue what happened this evening, has he?' whispered Venus.

'Not as far as we know,' Dennis replied.

Marshall looked out at the vast sea of faces.

'Wow,' he gasped.

Everyone laughed.

'I know I can ramble on sometimes,' he admitted, 'but tonight I'm going to keep this incredibly short. I want to welcome you all and I want to thank you all. There are far too many people to mention here tonight. It just goes to prove that making a film is a massive team effort. I've always been blessed with incredible teams and the one that worked on *Sword* was one of the most incredible I've ever met.'

There were cheers, whistles and thunderous applause.

Marshall held up his hand for quiet. 'That's the schmooze over,' he said, laughing, 'let's get on with this movie. I've only seen the whole thing once and that was with my two teenage sons, who talked the whole way through!'

There were more laughs and whistles.

'Enjoy it!' exclaimed Marshall. 'If you like it, tell me at the end. If you hate it, stay away!'

There was another massive wave of applause and Marshall stepped out of the spotlight. All lights faded and the huge curtains swished back as colour filled the screen.

SUNDAY

'Indigo was so messed up by her dad's death that she was actually going to *kill* Scott Marshall and his family?' asked Kate, taking a sip of water from her glass.

Kate and Venus were sitting up in Venus's bedroom, Kate on the bed and Venus on her desk chair.

'You can see it from her perspective,' replied Venus. 'I'm not excusing her in any way, but her family were totally destroyed when her dad was killed on that set.'

'You're right,' said Kate, nodding. 'Who knows how long she must have been planning this?' Kate shivered.

'I really liked Indigo,' said Venus. 'She seemed so friendly – and she was so talented.'

'What's next then, Venus? More stunt work?'

Venus laughed. 'Er . . . no. It's homework and school. Boring maths lessons – God, I *so* wish we had another week off.'

'Tell me about it.'

Venus was about to ask Kate about her plans when her mobile rang.

'Hi Jed, how're you?'

'Hi, I'm totally out of it. I went out with mates last night.'

'Good night?' Venus asked.

'It was cool,' he replied, 'but it would have been better if you were there. Anyway, forget me, how was the premiere?'

'Totally amazing,' Venus replied.

'Chat to Saffron or any of the A-list?'

'Of course!' said Venus, laughing. 'And the paparazzi wouldn't let me leave the red carpet!'

'What about the rest of the day – any drama?'

Venus paused. Her mind raced with images of Elliot toppling backwards off the roof of *Le Cadre*, Indigo's enraged face, the bomb . . .

'Nothing special,' she replied. 'Just chilling out really.'

Twenty minutes later, Venus pushed open a café door and walked inside. The smell of roasted coffee beans and freshly baked croissants filled her nostrils and tantalised her tastebuds. Sidestepping a row of tables filled with chattering work colleagues and dating couples, she headed for a blue door at the back of the café. This led out on to a short flight of stone steps that took her up to a square patio decked with honey-coloured strips of wood. Colourful plants hung from baskets along the low wooden fence surrounding the patio, and the far wall, where the fence was a lot higher, was covered in ivy.

Elliot was sitting at the furthest table, flicking through a paper. He stood up when Venus approached, smiled broadly and gave her a hug.

'Recovered from yesterday?' he asked, his face displaying concern.

'I think so,' replied Venus.

They sat down and, almost immediately, a waitress appeared. Elliot ordered a cappuccino and a Danish pastry; Venus asked for a grapefruit juice and a piece of apple strudel.

'I've got to leave for my flight in three hours,' said Elliot.

Venus felt a tug in her chest. 'Can't you stay a bit longer?' she said quietly. 'I mean, just so we could spend a bit more time together that doesn't involve criminal investigation, scaling walls and chucking bombs in rivers?'

Elliot laughed. 'Our time together has been pretty crazy, hasn't it? I feel really guilty for getting you involved in something that turned out to be so dangerous. We haven't exactly been doing the usual father-and-daughter activities. But in terms of returning to the States, I have no choice. I've got a job and I need to do it.'

They were silent for a few moments.

'I have no idea when I'm going to see you again,' said Venus, 'so I'd really like you to finish telling me what happened fourteen years ago. I've got a right to know.'

'First of all, you *will* be seeing me again,' answered Elliot, drumming his fingers on the table, 'and second, I agree, you do have a right to know.'

'So tell me,' said Venus.

Elliot took a deep breath, scratched his cheek and gazed across the table at his daughter. 'OK,' he said, 'I'm going to tell you, but there are some things which will probably upset you.'

'What, more than fourteen years of not seeing my own father?' Venus pointed out.

'Fair comment,' Elliot responded.

Venus leaned forward in her seat. She'd been waiting for an explanation for his departure her whole life and now he was about to finally tell her. The mere thought of this sent shivers down her spine.

'You already know that I used to work for the US Government. Like I said, I can't go into details about other aspects of my work, but I can tell you everything that relates to you, OK?'

Venus nodded.

'Well, fourteen and a bit years ago, there was a major drugs gang operating out of central London. They were a very tough, very ruthless outfit who killed whenever their interests were threatened. Some of my colleagues and I were sent over to investigate.'

'If the gang were working in London, why didn't the *British* police investigate them?' asked Venus, hanging on to every word.

'The British police *were* involved,' responded Elliot, 'but one of the two big bosses was a US citizen. The British authorities needed specialist American knowledge. That's why we got the call. We're talking about a *huge* drugs operation here, Venus, involving hundreds of different-ranking criminals. There were massive amounts of money at stake – I mean billions. When payments came in, these guys laundered the money all over the globe, using untraceable accounts and a never-ending list of aliases.'

'So you came over to arrest them?'

'No,' Elliot sighed, 'I came to join them.'

'To *join* them!' gasped Venus.

Elliot took a sip of his cappuccino. 'It was proving impossible to nail these guys,' he explained. 'They always managed to stay a couple of steps ahead of us. It was maddening, so the Americans and the British jointly decided that someone needed to *infiltrate* this gang. They felt it was the only way of securing some solid evidence against them.'

'And that meant you?'

Elliot nodded. 'We were all aware that this was an extremely dangerous strategy, but we couldn't see any other options. So I spent six months embedding myself in London's criminal underworld, getting to know the different characters – from the tiniest villains to the biggest players. I put my face about, spread tales of my impressive villainous past and waited.'

'What happened?'

'One day, I just *happened* to be in the right place at the right time. They were very suspicious of me at first and carried out loads of checks, but I'd made sure my name had been indelibly scorched on to the brains of the city's best-connected villains. The drugs gang bought my background and, a week later, I became their wheels.'

At that moment a waitress appeared at their table, carrying a tray with their drinks.

'Thanks,' said Elliot, waiting for her to disappear again before he continued.

'The bank job went as planned. It was a nasty business, but by very quick thinking I managed to save a security guard's life. It wasn't much, but it was better than nothing. The gang netted around ten million pounds. Everyone was ecstatic.'

'Sorry,' cut in Venus, 'but what's this got to do with Mum?'

'I'm coming to that bit,' replied Elliot. 'A couple of days

later, I met Gail outside the law college. I told you, it was sheer madness to get involved with her; a law student and an undercover agent who was in the thick of one of the world's most vicious crime syndicates!'

'But you started getting close.'

'Yes.'

'And you couldn't tell her about your job, right? You had to keep that part of your life completely secret?'

'Absolutely,' sighed Elliot. 'I started literally leading *two* lives – it was mad. Whenever the gang needed a driver, and sometimes this happened at the very last minute, I *had* to be there.'

'What did you tell Mum you did?'

'I said I was employed by the US Government and was often called away at very short notice. She accepted this. After all, it was true in a way.'

'And then?' asked Venus.

Elliot paused and took another sip of his cappuccino. 'And then, she got pregnant,' he said. 'It was a complete shock to both of us.'

'So you both flipped out?'

'Kind of, but we didn't lose touch with reality. We talked about it for hours and hours, and we both agreed that we were going to have this baby and put every effort into looking after you. I was all over the place. A very big part of me wanted to bow out of the gang immediately and do what I knew to be the right thing, i.e. be with you and your mum. But when I finally told my handler – the UK Government agent helping me – about my relationship with Gail and the fact she was pregnant, she went ballistic. She raged and screamed and accused me of jeopardising the whole operation.'

'Which was kind of true.'

'Exactly,' agreed Elliot. 'My handler demanded that I ditch Gail, baby or no baby. I refused point-blank and we had a massive stand-off. She was a really tough cookie by the name of Carla Radcliff.'

Venus's eyes widened. 'Radcliff!' she mouthed. 'That's how you and Dennis know her?'

Elliot nodded.

'Radcliff applied pressure to you?' Venus asked.

'You can say that again,' replied Elliot quietly, 'but there was no way I was going to leave Gail. After a few days of rows and discussions with my handler, I agreed to stay in the gang until everyone was busted. But after that, I told them I would be settling in London to be with Gail and you, and that I'd be leaving my job. She accepted this compromise.'

'So . . . so what made you rush off like you did?'

Elliot pinched the bridge of his nose and closed his eyes for a few seconds. 'Something went very badly wrong with the operation,' he answered, opening his eyes as a dark look crossed his face. 'I was ordered to leave London with an hour's notice. I was with a woman and a three-month-old baby who meant everything to me, and yet there I was being told to leave them. So I refused.'

'Presumably Radcliff didn't agree to that?'

'She said if I didn't leave the country immediately, it was pretty certain that my life would be in serious danger, in addition to the lives of many others – and that included you and Gail.'

Venus tried to say something, but nothing came out of her mouth.

'Leaving you and your mum was the most appalling thing I've ever done, and believe me I've done some pretty bad things,' said Elliot, 'but there was no way on earth I was going to endanger the lives of the woman I loved and my only child. So I got on a plane and flew out of England, planning to come back to London a few days later.'

'But you didn't come back then, did you?' whispered Venus.

'At first Radcliff told me I couldn't have any contact with Gail. She monitored me. I mean, I was working for her and *she* was spying on *me*. It was mad! When I finally got the all-clear, I flew straight over. But Gail refused to talk to me. Six weeks had passed without a word from me and she'd assumed I'd died in a gutter somewhere.'

'Why didn't you just tell her the truth?'

'I did! Or at least I tried to. But she wasn't having it. I'd left her in her greatest hour of need, and in her book that was completely unforgivable. I tried to explain the situation and promised her we could sort things out. But she was totally traumatised by my abrupt departure. She wouldn't let me in. I phoned her, I wrote to her, I tried everything I could think of, but I made no progress. She told me to stay away from her and our child, and never to turn up in your lives again.'

'So how come you get on with Radcliff now? Why don't you hate her?'

Elliot sighed. 'I did hate her for a while, but at the end of the day, I realised she was right. She probably saved my life, and Gail's life – and your life.'

Venus's temples throbbed. It felt like her entire life history had suddenly been re-written.

But Elliot wasn't finished. 'For the next year, I kept on trying to contact Gail. I begged, I pleaded, I cajoled, but she wasn't having it. You know how steely she can be. She wasn't going to change her mind – whatever I said or did. As far as she was concerned, I'd betrayed her and that was that.'

'But what about the dangers you'd have faced if you'd stayed? What about the fact that your staying would have placed her and me in danger? Couldn't she see you'd been put in an impossible situation?'

'She was furious with me; she said I should never have got involved with her – I was infiltrating a drugs gang, for God's sake! She said my job should have prevented me from striking up a relationship with her. And she was right, I should never have asked her out – it was stupid, it was selfish. Don't be angry with Gail,' said Elliot. 'She had every right to reject me. I left her at a terribly difficult time.'

Venus rubbed her eyes and drank some of her juice. This was all incredibly hard to take in. Gail had never told her any of this; she'd always maintained that Elliot had walked out with *no explanation* and *never bothered to get in touch again*. But, assuming that Elliot was telling the truth, this meant that *Gail* had been lying to her for all these years.

'In the end,' Elliot went on, 'she got an injunction against me contacting her. When that came through, I finally accepted defeat. You were about fifteen months old at the time and that was the end of my trying to stay in touch with her. I went back to the States, defeated and distraught.' A smile grew across Elliot's lips. 'But through Dennis I knew about every test you'd taken, every race you'd run and I have the full picture of your life as a stunt girl. I'm really proud of everything you've done.'

Venus felt hot tears slipping down her cheeks, and wiped them with the sleeve of her fleece.

'This job presented the perfect opportunity; I wasn't going to live my whole life letting you think I just walked out on you and never tried to see you again. I may have made lots of mistakes in my life, but giving up on you wasn't going to be one of them.'

Venus took another sip. She was about to ask him more about his life in the States when she suddenly became aware of a small commotion somewhere behind her. The waitress who'd served them was remonstrating with someone.

'There are no more tables out there,' the waitress insisted, 'I've already told you.'

But this didn't deter the customer, who sidestepped the waitress and strode straight up and out on to the decking.

Venus spun round and her face contorted in shock.

Striding across the decking was her mum.

Gail's eyes and Elliot's eyes were locked on each other's like prize-fighters assessing each other.

Venus's mouth dropped open.

For once in her life, she was totally speechless.